Coasting down the street in the semi-darkness, punctuated by the golden-yellow light of the old-fashioned lampposts, Lissa's hands shook at the wheel. *Which way did I come in?* The homes at Golden Meadows sat just outside of Pinewood in a borough called Elmdale. By day, this wouldn't be an issue. Now, at dusk, the world took on an unfamiliar patina.

Her mind spun. *Lacy, where are you?* The creepy image of the white SUV suddenly came to mind again, and she shivered at the thought that she'd been followed here. He could be parked outside like the other cars and snatched Lacy when she came to wait at the curb. He could have enticed her with candy or...? Lissa didn't want to think about it. Then the maintenance guy, Mike Hemstead, flew into her head. He seemed innocuous with the cover of having a little girl. Double life? A pervert? Lissa shook off the thoughts.

Frantically, she scanned the area. Her eyes darted back and forth checking both sides of the street. The last house in the development sat on the crest of a hill above a scruffy patch of untended land adjacent to a grove of trees. Beyond the owner's property line, she glimpsed something. There. *What was that?* She slammed her foot on the brake and strained in the low light for what caught her attention. Empty beer cans and fast food wrappers littered the clearing at the edge of the development. She set the parking brake and jumped out. She ran through the weeds and debris and braced at what she saw. Three holes and black markings took the shape of an eerie grin. *Lacy's costume.*

Beyond the Roses

by

Mary Cantell

Beyond the Roses

Cover Art by *Kim Mendoza*

The Wild Rose Press, Inc.
PO Box 708
Adams Basin, NY 14410-0708
Visit us at www.thewildrosepress.com

Publishing History
First Mystery Rose Edition, 2018
Print ISBN 978-1-5092-2324-4
Digital ISBN 978-1-5092-2325-1

Published in the United States of America

Dedication

To my beloved husband, my love always,
and to the memory of my precious mother,
who nurtured the writing bud in me, thank you.
Above all, to my Lord,
who guides my mind and heart to write.

Acknowledgements

Many thanks go to my wonderful editor, Judi Mobley, whose skills and wisdom led to the crafting of this story. Through so many months of working together, your faithfulness and support carried me to the finish line. You never wavered. Thanks for teaching me so much about the craft.

Thanks also goes to the great team of beta readers and editors at The Wild Rose Press who supported this project, and to my dear friend, Trayce Duran, thank you for your keen eye in helping to make the story shine all the more through your diligent efforts.

Thanks also go to the many people who lent their insight and knowledge:

Debra Culver, PennStar

John Gallagher, Penn Presbyterian Hospital

Lt. Michael Kochis, Alexandria Police Department

Kristi Michael, Frederick County Sheriff's Office

And the kind staff/personnel at:

Jefferson Hospital, Philadelphia

Mercy Suburban Hospital

Alexandria Sheriff's Office

Winchester Police Department

Maryland State Police Department

Frederick City, Maryland, Police Department

For my husband, Jeffrey James, thank you for allowing me to bore you with the details of every change in plot line and for your grace in listening at all hours, along with your timely input.

Teresa Mora McColgan, my friend, thank you, as always, for your prayers.

Beyond the Roses

The darker the night, the brighter the stars, the deeper the grief, the closer is God.

~ *Fyodor Dostoyevsky*

Chapter One

Bryn Mawr, Pennsylvania
March 4th, 2005

Twelve boxes the color of creamed coffee filled
half the tiny living room, all labeled in bold black
marker as to their contents. Lissa dropped the thirteenth
one on the floor and heaved a sigh at the growing
eyesore cluttering the formerly pristine space.
Bittersweet thoughts circled in her mind like crows
descending. Another stab of sadness doused her spirit.
"I hate this," she mumbled under her breath, dreading
the whole idea of moving.

With her boss's recent transfer, an invitation to
follow him seemed like a good idea at first—a miracle,
actually—as her co-workers were not blessed with the
same fortune when the PR&D department of Merka
Pharmaceuticals downsized. They were sending out
resumes right about now. They thought her *lucky*,
though Lissa knew it was the Lord's blessing—not
luck—that she wouldn't have to worry where her rent
money would come from. Now, two weeks later, she
questioned her decision to accept his offer. Was this the
best choice for her family? Uprooting her life and that
of her daughter's—for a job? There were plenty of
administrative positions in the pharmaceutical industry
in suburban Philadelphia, but Dr. Billing was the

kindest boss she ever had, and she cornered the market salary-wise. Still, a nagging thought poked at her: unpack everything and forget the whole idea.

Overheated from shuffling boxes all morning, she went to the living room window and lifted the sash to let in some fresh air. The morning sun shone hazily through a strand of opal clouds. She leaned in to let the drift of cool air slip over her face. With her eyes closed, she pictured the boxes gone and her worries about the move drifting up and away into the clouds. She breathed deeply, in and out…she couldn't get enough of the rich bourbon scent. *A neighbor's pile of burning leaves?* As she lingered in her thoughts, the doorbell buzzed. Lissa inhaled the ambrosia one more time before lowering the sash and going to the door.

"Hey, Robin," she said brightly. Her mood lightened at the surprise visit of her best friend from church, along with her little boy.

"Hey, hope we're not interrupting too much. Just came to say g'bye." Robin held up a tiny purple gift bag topped with a mound of silver and purple ribbons. "For Lacy."

"Oh, how sweet of you; come on in." Lissa lifted her hand to sweep her unruly bangs out of her eyes and pulled open the door, embarrassed at the glut of disarray. "I apologize for the mess," she said, waving her arm up and down. Between the packed and half-packed boxes, along with strewn newspapers, rolls of masking tape, and general disorder, Lissa cringed, hating her sense of order disturbed. It was as though navigating the way along a ship's deck in a hurricane. Unsure. Insecure. She moved toward the hall and called, "Lacy, Miss Robin is here. Alex, too. Come say goodbye, honey." She took the shiny purple bag and placed it daintily on a clear spot on top of the entryway table. "It's lovely, Robin. Lacy loves anything purple, thank you," she chirped and gestured toward the sofa. "Have a seat."

Robin plopped herself down and helped Alex unzip his jacket. "So did you find out which office you'll be working out of?" Robin asked, tugging on the zipper.

"Gaithersburg," she said, her hands on her hips. "It's one of the satellite branches. Near my old hometown."

"That's great," Robin replied with little enthusiasm. "I loved Maryland. Daddy was stationed there for a while." She offered a strained smile. Alex shrugged off his jacket as Robin's face morphed into a palette of emotion that tugged at Lissa's heart.

"Hey, what's the matter?" Lissa consoled, knowing her friend's sensitive nature. Lissa understood what it was like to wear her heart on her sleeve. She was the same way and could well up with emotion just witnessing someone's good fortune at winning the grand prize on a TV game show. Feeling much like she was watching the game show winner now, she held it together—until tears pricked her eyes.

"Oh, nothin'," Robin muttered with a dismissive wave of her hand, shaking her head which sent her hair—a long cascade of dark tendrils—quivering across her cheeks.

"Aw…" Lissa leaned in and wrapped her arms around her. "…you'll be all right." A trace of White Shoulders sifted the air.

"Just that I'll be losin' a friend." Robin lifted her eyebrows expressively, seeming resigned to the loss.

Her syrupy drawl made the words all the more depressing. They'd been friends for years and were as close as the best of sisters, sharing everything from heartbreak to recipes.

"I feel the same way," Lissa replied, quickly swatting away a tear. "But after all you've done for me over the years...taking care of Lacy and everything." Lissa forced a smile. "There's no way it'll be out of sight out of mind with us, you know that. I'll keep in touch until you're sick of hearing from me." A light chuckle filled in when she ran out of words. She turned her attention to Alex, who stood politely at the foot of the couch, and she knelt to meet the sweet boy eye-to-eye. "Hey, buddy, why don't you go to Lacy's room and play together?" She pointed toward the hallway and then ruffled his crop of dirty blond hair. "Sound good?"

In a heartbeat, he darted down the hall. Halfway there, he turned around. "Can I go to the bathroom?"

"Of course, little man, it's on the left," she said and pointed down the hall, watching his little figure until he found it. She turned back to Robin. "Can I get you something?"

Robin shook her head. "Nope, we're all good. Just wanted to say our last farewell is all." She reached into her purse and brought out a package of tissues. "I didn't know you used to live in Maryland," she said, lifting one out.

Lissa plunked down on the sofa. "I thought I told you that?"

"Oh, you might have," Robin said, pressing the tissue to her nose. "Menopause is catching up with me. I sometimes forget my own name."

Lissa gave her a sympathetic nod and hoped her

own menopause years wouldn't be coming anytime soon. "Yep, good 'ol Pinewood," she said breezily. "Just a good old-fashioned town bordering Cherrydale and Pleasantville a few miles south of the Mason-Dixon Line. I don't remember even hearing a police siren. Well, maybe once."

Robin lifted an eyebrow curiously. "Some place. Sounds like a Norman Rockwell painting."

"It was," she said as a warm feeling rose at the memory of walking through one of the "kissing bridges" as they were called. Images of Pinewood's pastoral charm floated in and out of her mind. The rolling hills, the old covered bridges, the quaint homes and unruffled serenity. "Not quite a one-stoplight town but it had that same feel—at least, it used to. Who knows what it's like now. Don't get me wrong, we had our troubles, pranksters and stuff. Like the time this kid, Billy Underwood—wild kid, for sure—anyway, he let a snake loose inside the lingerie department of Starn's Bridal Shop. Crazy, right? And at Fielding's Feed and Farm store, this rambunctious dog got away from his owner and knocked over an entire rack of packed egg cartons. *Splat*...right on the floor." Lissa grinned, hoping the anecdotes would lighten Robin's spirit.

Robin gave her a curious look. "That's it, just snakes and dogs?"

"What can I say?" Lissa managed a shrug. "It was a backwoods town."

Robin rolled her eyes. "You've led a sheltered life, girl."

Lissa threw her hands up. "Just lucky, I guess."

They sat in silence, and Lissa took a mental snapshot of the moment: The sweet notes of jasmine sifting from Robin's perfume, the absence of the usual mild chaos emanating from Lacy's bedroom. Apparently, the children were playing quietly for a change.

"Well," Lissa said with a lazy smile, "I guess this is it." She let the words settle and hoped neither of them would cry again. "You've been such a good friend, Robin. I don't know who could have been more help to me after my mom's surgery and then her…" She bit back the rest of her sentence, feeling a sense of remorse for her mother's passing. As an only child after her baby brother died, the relationship with her beloved mother cemented into a tight-knit bond that nothing could unravel.

"That's what friends are for," Robin said. She cast her still glassy gaze around the room. "Well, I guess you've still got some more to do. Is there anything I can help you with?"

"Actually, I think we're pretty good." Lissa gave the room a quick glance. "Oh, wait." She held up a finger. "On second thought, there is something you can help me with. That is, if you wouldn't mind taking some food."

She went to the kitchen. Standing at the refrigerator, she called, "Would you have need of this?" She thrust an unopened quart of 2% milk out for Robin to see at the doorway. "I have some other things in here that you might want. Come take a look." She beckoned.

"Mom, Mrs. Logan," Alex's tiny voice rang with urgency as he ran up the hallway.

"We're in here, buddy," Lissa called from the kitchen.

Alex approached the threshold and looked up with

a question on his face. He cocked his head like a puppy, slipping his hands into his back pockets. "I don't know where Lacy is… I can't find her."

"You can't find Lacy?" Lissa said, perplexed. "Are you guys playing hide-and-seek?"

Alex slowly shook his head, his big blue saucer-eyes forlorn.

"Hmmm, that's weird." She put down the jar of pickles on the counter and yelled, "Lacy?"

Silence.

Lissa cocked her head toward the hallway. "Honey, where are you?" She struggled to keep worry from her voice and scurried down the corridor of the rented duplex to her daughter's bedroom. Finding it empty, she checked her own room farther down the hall, along with the bathroom and the hallway closet before coming back to the kitchen. *Where is she?* Lissa hustled to the living room and yanked up the blinds. A stream of dust floated in the sun-filtered air. She opened the window wide and strained to catch any sign of her daughter in the backyard. The picnic table, empty. The swings, still. The woods beyond the fence loomed ominously like silent warriors. *Did Lacy go for a walk? Or somehow get lost?* There were too many hiding places for a small girl or predator. Thoughts of her deceased husband Jason came to mind, and with all that she'd lost, she couldn't lose Lacy, too.

Her stomach hollowed. Worry strangled her words. "She's not here. Where could she—" Without verbally completing her thought, she bolted for the front door.

"Maybe she's out front," Robin said, following out to the portico where Lissa held a hand to her eyes to shield the piercing sunrays coming out from behind the clouds. Robin followed Lissa's lead and cast her eyes toward the opposite end of the street. "Where could she be, Liss?"

"I don't know," Lissa said, her voice wobbly. "She's never left the house before without telling me."

She paced stiffly from one side of the stone portico to the other, hoping this was just a case of unnecessary concern, and she'd turn around and Lacy would be there. Gripped with worry, she quickly surveyed the front yard still not recovered from the austere frost of winter. The dead winter-brown lawn. Twiggy bare barberry bushes. In the semi-quiet of mid-morning, a rustling sound caught her attention. Squirrels. She ran around to the big oak tree at the side of the house marking the edge of the property. The tire swing hanging from the lower branch hung still. The hammock, empty.

The sound of a child's voice pierced the air. Lissa turned abruptly to see a white van zoom down the quiet residential street. Did the voice come from inside the van? A sudden shock hit like a freight train at the thought of Lacy inside. The story of a white van circling the neighborhood last summer came to mind. A man at the wheel. The rumor was that he'd lured kids into the back with the offer of free tickets to the Baltimore Orioles' games. Lissa pictured her free-spirited daughter lolling down the street in her bouncy step, oblivious to the dangers around her.

Her only child, Lacy often spent time alone. Lissa found comfort looking out the window seeing her playfully engaged, either having a pretend picnic or tea with her Barbie dolls on the hammock in the summer. The child's independent nature ran in the family—

somewhere. Her daughter's free spirit coupled with Lissa's worry-prone nature created a less than cohesive mix. She tried to control her fears by talking to the counselor about it at Lacy's school. The woman gave some helpful advice: *try to think like a child... they are so curious—about everything... they aren't cognizant of the importance of time or what adults find important... give them their space, etc.* As much as Lissa tried to apply what she learned from the counselor, the lessons often stayed in her head—rarely reaching her heart.

The once peaceful morning turned ominous in Lissa's world, and she wondered how she could have thought the neighborhood was ever safe. With her heart pulsing in double time, she double checked the back yard again and studied every inch of the property—the rickety, splintered fence, the tall imposing trees.

Lissa berated herself for being too preoccupied earlier in the morning with packing and boxing up the kitchen and linen closet items. She mentally retraced her steps and struggled to remember when she last saw Lacy. After breakfast, she cleared the table, rinsed the leftover milk from their cereal bowls and dribbles of orange juice from their glasses, and picked up where she left off to continue boxing their belongings. She had so much to do and so little time to do it; her mind kept buzzing with the next thing on the list. The movers were scheduled for tomorrow. How did the child slip out without being noticed?

Two hours later and shortly before noon, still no sign of Lacy. Lissa had contacted all the neighbors she knew. They canvassed the neighborhood from the tiny strip mall at the corner to the playground at Elmwood Park. Later, the group reconvened on the sidewalk, all bearing long, desperate faces. A frantic Lissa lifted her cell phone and was one second away from calling the police when the figure of a little girl appeared in the distance. *Lacy?* Lissa's heavy heart lifted as though a sodden weight fell away as her daughter came loping across the neighbor's lawn. Seeing her daughter's gazelle-like dexterity, she delighted at the child's athleticism. Her immense joy overrode any indiscretion Lacy could ever muster.

"Lacy," she cried as her daughter approached. Cheers erupted from the make-shift search party of neighbors Lissa had corralled. "Honey, we were worried," Lissa said, about to cry from joy as she reached out to hug her. A sweet blend of grape-flavored bubble gum and baby shampoo scented the air where Lacy stood.

"Debbie let me—" Lacy panted, "—she let me play her CDs, Mom." She stopped to take an expansive breath. "All of them," she bubbled excitedly. "And we drank sodas and everything."

"You should have asked my permission, honey." Lissa's brow knit. "You know better than to leave the house without letting Mommy know, right?" She pushed stray strands of cherry-brown hair out of Lacy's eyes. "I'm serious, Lacy. Please don't ever do that again." The commanding tone of her on-the-spot mini-lecture faded in light of the news her daughter was safe. It could have been worse. Lacy could have been hurt or—worse. Lissa didn't want to think about the things she heard on the news. Or the van.

"I'm sorry, Mom," she said with a shrug, the earlier enthusiasm quickly dampened.

"It's okay now," Lissa said as Robin reached for

Lacy's arm and gave a gentle squeeze.

"You're safe," Robin said, "and that's all that matters."

"Yes," said Grace, their next-door neighbor, as they all nodded in agreement "That's all that matters."

Soon Lissa would take her daughter away from her home, just as her own mother had done those many years ago. She'd made a valiant effort to be a good parent—both mother and father to her after Lissa's father's death. Now she planned to do the same. It would be a good thing, Lissa tried to convince herself, even though Lacy would have to start fresh with a new school, move into a classroom already in full swing, and make new friends. She wondered if her daughter was telling her in some way that she didn't want to go? Lissa was about to retrace her steps back to the place where she spent the better part of childhood. The safe and quiet streets of Pinewood, Maryland. Where nothing bad ever happened.

Chapter Two

On her last evening before the move, Lissa slipped into her pajamas after dinner and settled down in front of the computer. She checked her email first and then Facebook. A picture of a group of children popped up on her wall posted from an old school friend. *Here's a throwback from the past*, Katie Knox wrote. Intrigued, Lissa tried to make out the faces in the grainy photo.

Children from her old elementary school back in Pinewood and not much older than her own daughter stood around Principal Golden's brand new white Triumph Spitfire convertible after the school's May Day Fun Night. She remembered the time well. Everyone was impressed with the car and made a fuss over it. With her rotund derriere and sensible low-heeled shoes, Miss Golden looked more fit for a practical midsize vehicle than the sporty Spitfire. Lissa, warmed by the nostalgia, chuckled out loud at the incongruity of it all.

"What is it, Mom?" Lacy dropped what she was doing on the floor and hopped onto her lap.

"It's a picture of when I was a little girl, sweetie." Lissa mused how much Lacy resembled her at the same age with their similar features and auburn hair. "There I am, see?"

"Who's that boy standing next to you?" Lacy pressed a finger to the screen.

Her voice turned soft. "That's my old friend, Brian." Lissa delighted at even saying his name out loud.

"He's cute," Lacy drawled. "Did you like him?"

Lissa was caught off guard. *Whoa... really, Lacy?* A bit flustered, she replied, "Brian Pickering?" Her voice came out high-pitched, a sure sign of uneasiness, but hopefully, Lacy wouldn't pick up on it.

"Pickering?" Lacy giggled. "That's a funny name."

Lissa frowned and spoke as though defending his family's honor. "No, it's not." She hoped she didn't give herself away. *Of course I liked him.*

On a balmy spring evening twenty-six years ago, Lissa tried to get her school crush Brian Pickering's attention, particularly when some of the kids began playing board games in one of the upstairs classrooms during the school's annual Fun Night, and she went looking for him. Sadly, that night he paid more attention to the tall and leggy Patti Cotter, her budding beauty already commanding, even at ten years old. The hot sting of envy filled Lissa upon realizing Brian didn't even notice her disappointment.

Every gym class during the winter when it was too cold to enjoy the outdoors, her classmates joined some of the other grades for a big square dance in the cafeteria. All the while she pined to dance with him or to touch the blond bristles on the back of his freshly cut hair, she'd been stuck with the fawning attention of another boy in her class. Donny McCall. Whenever she glanced in Brian's direction, there stood freckle-faced Donny gazing up at her with his squinty eyes wanting to be her partner. He was a sweet kid, but his hands slithered in hers like two wet clams. Saying *no, thanks* to the poor soul would have broken his spirit. Someone like fancy classmate Sue Ellen Clanton, who tied her hair with shiny ribbons resembling a prized poodle, would have no trouble telling Donny *no.*

Gazing at the computer screen, Lissa marveled how the picture made it to Facebook after all these years. The picture resurfaced moments later with some added comments: *"Look at that hair… Wow, that car is probably a collector's item by now."* Names from her past not thought of or heard from in decades appeared to join the conversation one-by-one. She typed in her own comment—*"good times."*

After Lissa tucked Lacy into bed, she went back to the computer and, once again, lingered on the old group photo. Curious as to how Brian turned out, she went to his Facebook page and clicked through the pictures he posted of himself with friends and family. There were two little girls—both quite pretty—and a woman in his life—most likely his wife. Lissa felt like a voyeur sifting through the pictures, as though she were intruding into his personal space.

Her grade school days with him floated back… the tall kangaroo he sculpted in clay during art period when everyone else molded scrawny snakes or turtles… the after school club he started and invited her, the only girl, to join after she won the President's Physical Fitness Award for most athletic girl in fourth grade, and the reading comprehension tests where Brian soared to the top level, leaving the rest of the class behind. Her pulse ticked faster, and a warm feeling came over her as she turned off the computer and went to bed. Brian Pickering was the last thing on her mind as she drifted to sleep.

Chapter Three

Pinewood, Maryland
March 5, 2005

The well-kept homes, each as lovely as the next, resembled page layouts out of *House Beautiful* magazine. Southern charm influenced the neighborhood right down to the tulip beds, Lissa thought, as she browsed through the manicured lawns and landscaping of the homes for rent in the Pinewood County website. She settled on an old Victorian on Bellevue Avenue offering a second-floor apartment and located not far from where she once lived.

"And here are the bedrooms," the elderly landlady, Miss Rucker, announced as she plodded down the narrow hallway smelling of old varnish, her dowager's hump popping through her pale lace sweater.

The furnished unit had a stone fireplace and an exposed brick wall. For the low rent—a godsend. The place was good enough with just enough space and privacy for her and Lacy, though the tiny kitchen with its passé avocado color scheme and stained sink didn't lend much appeal. That, along with the rumor of a haunted house in the neighborhood, were the only drawbacks. A mason jar next to the sink held some greasy looking wooden utensils, and a dusty spice rack void of spice jars hung on the wall next to an old model

Freeze-king refrigerator. *How long had it been there?* Even though the kitchen was old, Lissa knew that after a bucket of hot water and a thorough soapy cleaning, the room could gain back some of its luster.

What drew her most in selecting the property was the formal garden adjacent to a large protective stone wall enclosing the property. The lifelike pictures of the garden in full bloom on the internet were stunning. A small pond sat at the bottom of the hill like a shiny jade coin.

After the tour, they went down to Miss Rucker's apartment where she brought out the lease agreement paperwork. The décor in the dim sitting room in the lower half of the house where Miss Rucker and her mother lived reminded Lissa of her great-grandmother and namesake, Melissa Rose Leads, a society matron from Macon, Georgia. She owned similar furniture like the commanding mahogany desk set with carved finials that sat on the far wall surrounded by a brocade sofa, loveseat, and two button-back pink velvet chairs. A marble-topped table held a crystal lamp topped with china figurines set in a circle. A large statue of Mary, the blessed mother, stood in the corner. Miss Rucker set the papers on the table by the fireplace and turned on the lamp, which cast a circle of gold light on the lace-shrouded table. Lissa slung the strap of her handbag over the back of the chair, took a seat, and moved the papers closer while reaching backward into her purse for her glasses.

"They keep the mice in check," Miss Rucker said to Lacy with a wink and introduced the cats to her as she sat giggling on the floor, charmed with their attention. Tingo and Tango purred and rubbed up against Lacy while Miss Rucker's third cat, Theodore, skulked around the room meowing as though disturbed by the intrusion or jealous of the bonding he wasn't receiving. Miss Rucker's beige and white Shih Tzu kept a keen dog eye on all of them from the corner. *Mice?* Lissa paused for a second before continuing to read the fine print. *Great.*

Lacy continued to run the palm of her hand across the heads of the black and white felines and quickly bonded with Tingo and Tango.

"Miss Rucker, I have a question," Lacy said, cocking her head. "Is there a haunted house around here?"

With a scowl, the woman quickly shook her head, "Oh, no," she said, sounding affronted. "Well, at least, I certainly hope not."

"I heard there was," Lacy replied, pawing the cats.

"In this neighborhood?" She clutched her pearl necklace and nervously stroked it.

Lacy nodded and then shrugged. "I don't remember what street, though," and Lissa wished her daughter hadn't mentioned it.

"Miss Rucker," Lissa interjected apologetically, "Lacy read something about it online, on my computer. I must have left my screen open to the real estate website where your house is listed." She waved as though dismissing the idea. "The real estate lady who recommended your place didn't know about it either…it's not a problem just a curiosity."

"Mom, what about Amityville?" Lacy cocked her head again.

"Oh, right. I lived in Amityville, New York, one summer after college." Lissa began. "I stayed on Ocean

Avenue, you know, where there was this house that became famous for being haunted. I'm surprised you remembered the town's name, Lace."

"It's a movie," Lacy added, smartly.

"Yes, honey, but it's all speculation," Lissa replied with the calm but firm tone of laying the matter to rest and not wanting to further rattle Miss Rucker.

"Frankly, I believe haunted houses are nothing more than people's imaginations," Miss Rucker piped in with conviction.

"I agree, Miss Rucker." She gave an affirmative nod.

"Imaginations coupled by a marketing plan," Miss Rucker added with a titter as she scowled and shook her head while adjusting one of the bobby pins in her steel gray bun.

"We should only believe half of what we see and even less of what we hear," Lissa began. "I used to walk the dog of my neighbor—Mrs. Elmore—dear lady, and she would come to her door always wearing a nightgown. They're all she ever wore," she continued. "And a thick scent of sweet Emeraude hung in the air whenever she opened the door—and even after it was closed. They said the poor soul suffered from an incurable disease and was forced to mask the odor by drenching herself in heavy perfume. The tea-toting busybodies in the neighborhood labeled her *a woman of the evening*. Can you imagine?" Lissa frowned and Miss Rucker clucked disapprovingly. "Anyway, so much for the truth among fiction." Lissa looked pointedly at Lacy. "Including haunted houses, young lady."

Miss Rucker moved to the window. "My, oh my,"

she murmured, staring outside. In mid-sentence she suddenly stopped short. "Oh, dear."

Her eyes remained fixed toward the outside where airy clouds stretched across the postcard-pretty morning sky as Lissa looked up, wondering what attracted the woman's attention. "Is everything all right, Miss Rucker?"

"Oh, yes, I'm fine. Everything is all right," Miss Rucker said, turning away quickly. Her eyes bounced around the room as though she'd lost control and didn't know where to focus. A thin line drew on her lips. "Quite all right."

Lissa sat up straighter, attempting to raise her sight line to catch a glimpse out the window, hoping to pick up on whatever it was that made the woman break character. Thick pines surrounding the park across the street and a man wearing a red baseball cap rounding the corner of the sidewalk were all she could see from her present angle. Getting up and running to the window wouldn't be appropriate, she reasoned. Unless there was some kind of danger. *Was there?* No, she reasoned, and went back to the paperwork. After reading the entire lease, she signed and dated the document and handed both copies back to the landlady who, in turn, signed them and gave one back to her along with the key.

"This is fine, yes, quite fine, indeed," Miss Rucker said. "It will be so nice having you and your daughter stay here." She smiled and cupped her quivering hands together. "Now, if there's anything you need or any questions you have, I'm only a floor away."

"Thank you, Miss Rucker," Lissa said, reaching for her handbag. "We'll be sure to let you know of any concerns we have."

"I hope you don't have many." The woman tittered.

Lissa hoped so, too, still wondering what could have upset Miss Rucker.

Chapter Four

"Yes, sir, I'll fax them right away. And the memo is ready to go. Dr. Fitzwater just signed off on it." Lissa stepped out of Dr. Billing's office and went back to her desk. She printed out the paperwork and went to the copy room. After sorting, collating, and copying the reports, she faxed her boss's requested information and went back to her desk. Settling down with a cup of Darjeeling tea, she checked her email and then opened Facebook. Her heart lightened at seeing a message from Brian Pickering. After all these years, she never expected to be in touch with someone from grade school, much less him. *Hmmm, what's this about?*

Brian: "Glad to hear you'll be coming back to the area. When you get settled, give me a shout. Maybe we can do lunch or coffee or something?" *A date?*

She replied: "Hi, Brian. Good to hear from you. I'm already here in Pinewood."

Seconds later, he wrote, "Cool. Pick a day and get back to me. My schedule is flexible."

"Sounds like a plan. Will do."

Will do? She cringed at rereading her choice of words. Sounded like the overly solicitous reply she would say to Dr. Billing, though she didn't recall ever saying it before.

He wants to see me? I thought he was married?

For the rest of the day, pleasant thoughts of Brian

swirled in her head. As much as she tried to focus on her work, a mental picture of him kept popping up like an unruly child. Everyone in her extended family knew about Brian. Dropping his name so often over the years, they all were familiar with his story. Even her late husband Jason once remarked jokingly that if he went on an overseas tour with his unit and didn't come back, she had his official permission to remarry. *"Maybe you'll get to marry Brian after all,"* he once said with a wink.

There was no one who could replace her handsome husband, first lieutenant Jason Logan, though Brian Pickering would be a close second. Brian moved swiftly up the government ladder and became the Chief of Security at the Department of Defense in Washington, D.C. before he was thirty.

Her mind wandered back to Brian's invitation. She didn't want to seem too forward and give him the idea she was desperate, so she played it cool. She waited until the following day to write back and consulting her boss's calendar, suggested the second Tuesday in April for their lunch date. Hopefully, by then the temperature would be warmer and the snow gone. A bubble of joy lifted in her heart at the thought of seeing him again and, like a giddy school girl, she floated her way through the rest of the day.

****

Whoosh...splat. The snowball landed squarely on the car window, nearly missing Lissa's eye. She stiffened at the cold flecks of ice that bounced off the glass. There was barely any snow left, just the plowed remains piled at the edge of the shopping center's parking lot. This late in the season, she didn't think getting hit with a snowball would be possible, let alone so soon after coming to a new neighborhood. *Was this the new hazing for those who just moved in? Greetings, and welcome to our fair town. Lovely.*

The alarm of almost being blinded turned to anger, and she promptly swept ice crystals from her coat lapels. Her temperature rose, releasing a flush of warmth under her woolen scarf, and she whipped her head around to follow the trajectory of the snowball. In front of the grocery store, shoppers shuffled in and out, and a particular set of individuals captured her attention: a group of boys making a mad dash around the corner. *Guilty.* She wanted to catch up with them, but their speed gave them a leg up on her. It would be too difficult to confront them now, though one thing gave them away. A towheaded boy towered over the others. His platinum locks shone like a lighthouse beacon above his navy blue parka. She'd seen him before.

Lissa opened the car door and slid in, muttering under her breath. *Stupid kids.* Lacy huddled close to the window drawing a smiley face on the glass. "What happened, Mom?"

"Some boys up to no good, that's all." She checked her eye in the rearview mirror. "They almost knocked my eye out with a snowball."

"Who were they?"

"I don't know, but I'm sure going to find out."

Lissa let out a sigh and started the car. The image of a shabby white clapboard in need of a good coat of paint popped into her head. The house stuck out over the others as it looked more like the *before* picture on a street of *afters*. Lissa remembered the tall boy in the front yard standing by the open hood of an old yellow jalopy during her jog through the neighborhood not long after moving in. Loud metallic music blared from the car's radio. If she hadn't slipped on a patch of black ice in front of the house and landed on her backside, almost losing her shoe in the process, she probably wouldn't have noticed him. How embarrassing, she had thought, hoping no one witnessed the incident.

Many of the homes on the neighboring streets featured prominent wrap-around porches and attracted her attention, and she especially loved the turrets. The residences reminded her of the great Victorian she stayed in one summer when working as a live-in nanny on Long Island right out of college.

"Before we go home, I'm going to make a stop," Lissa said, gripping the wheel tightly and loosening her scarf with her free hand. Traces of adrenaline still coursed through her veins at the thought of the snowball smacking her face. Fortunately, she'd had her sunglasses on.

"Where are we going, Mom?"

"Not far," she assured. Lissa kept her tone light and upbeat for the sake of her daughter. She knew Lacy was sensitive, never wanting to rock the boat or bring any conflict to a situation, and she wondered if this was the best thing to do in front of her. With her affable spirit, Lacy could make friends with anyone and would do so at any cost rather than make an enemy.

"I'm just going to speak to someone is all," she said, hoping her own tension hadn't spread to her daughter. She glanced back. "Nothing to be worried about," she confirmed.

A mantle of snow coating the lawns showcased the

neighborhood as crisply as a real estate brochure, rendering each of the houses a distinctive charm. Lissa canvassed a two-block area, trying to recall how to get to the house that loomed in her mind's eye. It was likely within a quarter to a half-mile away from her rental on Bellevue Avenue and somewhere along the jogging route she randomly chose for herself that wouldn't be too long or too strenuous to run.

Lissa drove toward Gallatin Street where charming Victorians stretched for most of the street. She turned at the third block onto Victoria Lane. *There.* She spotted the imposing presence on the corner and slowed the car. Overgrown bushes loomed below the windows like curious onlookers eager to peer inside. A dusting of snow still covered some of the eaves, but the turret rose cleanly into the cold blue sky. An eerie vibe came from it, and she thought twice whether to follow through on her initial plan. A shiver ran through her.

She pulled to the curb across from a dilapidated picket fence. The mailbox hung precariously and appeared weighted under a large chunk of partially melted ice, rendering the worn letters stenciled in black barely legible. The visible ones spelled *ELLING.* There sat the old yellow car in the driveway, the one she first noticed the time she came this way before. A rush of guilt hit at the prospect of ratting out the boy, but he looked old enough to have known better and that he could have taken out someone's eye.

"Wait here, honey, I'll be right back." She glanced back to her daughter, who bore a worried expression.

Back in the car, Lissa shared what happened. "I spoke with his mother, and I explained to her the seriousness of the boy's actions. Throwing a snowball into someone's face is never good." Lissa hoped her words conveyed a lesson. "But it's all settled now." She turned on the engine. "Hey, I don't know about you, but I'm in the mood for a nice grilled cheese and a hot cup of tomato soup for lunch when we get home," she said to Lacy, who had her nosed pressed up against the window. "That house looks spooky," Lacy said as they pulled away.

Casting a glance over the snow covered lawn, she couldn't help but agree with her daughter. The house was off-putting. A chill ran through her.

Chapter Five

Just before eight a.m., the main drag in the heart of downtown Gaithersburg bloated like an over-packed parking lot. Lissa's fingers tightened on the steering wheel in frustration. A sallow face in the harsh outdoor light framed by a mane of hair that lent more to *burnt sienna* than the preferable *chestnut red* stared back at her from the rearview mirror. Do-it-yourself hair coloring was cheap, but now she regretted not spending the extra money on a professional application. She flinched at the sight of gray hairs sprouting along her widow's peak. *Lord, I'm only thirty-four.* Frustrated, she released her grip on the wheel and reached for the Starbucks coffee cup and downed a sip. She closed her eyes for a brief second waiting for the caffeine jolt to do its magic.

As if a good omen, the car in front of her moved. She coasted ten feet when the New Jersey driver ahead of her slowed again. She jammed her foot on the brake and let out a pointed sigh. *Oh, for Pete's sake, go already.* Her last vacation at the Jersey shore came to mind where her most pressing issue was finding the misplaced suntan lotion cap or deciding on pizza or sushi for lunch. Then her thoughts quickly turned to pristine Bermuda with its pink sand and turquoise water...if only she had the money. Lacy's private school tuition consumed most of her expendable income, so that vacation wouldn't be happening any time soon.

Up ahead, something flashed in the distance. Lissa placed the lipstick-stained cup back into the holder when the jarring scream of an ambulance from somewhere behind jolted her. In the momentary distraction, some coffee splashed out and scalded her hand, leaving a tan puddle on the console.

"Ooooouuuucch," she said, in pain from the sting of hot coffee; she quickly grabbed a tissue to mop up the spill.

"Looks like an accident, Mom," Lacy said, craning her neck to see out the window. The queue of cars ahead stretched in a snaking sea of brake lights as far as she could see.

"It probably is," she said, annoyed, and quickly switched the radio station from soft rock to the all news station to catch a traffic report.

"Can we listen to the music station?" Lacy whined from the back seat.

"Shhh," Lissa said, waving her hand, irritably. "The traffic report is coming up."

"Sorry," the child replied softly and slunk back into her seat. "But I'd rather hear music."

"So would I, Lace," she said, wiping the console crevice, irked at knowing some coffee leaked below where she couldn't reach. "But we need to hear the traffic report. And put your seatbelt on please." Lissa's ears perked when the reporter mentioned *a serious problem.* She stopped wiping long enough to catch the mention of a collision involving a trash truck on Franklin Avenue at Crescent Lane, a few blocks from Lacy's school. "Oh, great," she said under her breath.

"Of all the days." Today was her date with Brian, and she had a report to finish as well as a meeting to attend, all before 11:30 a.m.—the time she hoped to skip out early to make it to the restaurant in time.

Storefronts lining the hub of the downtown business district brightened in the early light like awakened sleepy eyes. Janelle's Day Spa, La Patisserie, and La Bella Moda nestled side-by-side among a health food store and a flower shop. A few clothing boutiques featured headless mannequins wearing the latest cutting-edge fashion she couldn't afford. Too often, Lissa whisked through this part of town to and from work leaving the kitschy shops and boutiques behind in a sweeping blur. Being a single mother rarely lent itself to taking in the scenery or spending extra money. She downed the last dregs of coffee as the molasses of cars ahead inched forward. *Finally.* She pressed her foot to the pedal and glanced at the LED clock on the dashboard. Only ten minutes late.

Lissa pulled around the murky green pond to the front entrance of Gaithers Country Day School, which also served as a day camp during the summer. The winding granite stairway leading into the sprawling institution that once served as an old Revolutionary War-era enclave stretched like an oversized accordion. Giant shade trees stood at allegiance as they flanked the three-story stone mansion in the shadows.

"All right, have a good day," she said to Lacy, who opened the door and promptly flew out. Her *I love you* met with the slam of the car door.

She watched her daughter happily bounce down the sidewalk in her new shorts and sneakers. Where the child picked up the spritely style of walking with an

29

overt spring in her heel was anyone's guess. She rolled down the window. "I'll pick you up after school at the usual time and place, okay?"

"'Kay, mom," Lacy called back. Her hair, held off her face with Little Princess clips, shone like a wave of pennies in the early morning light.

Lissa waited until the child made her way safely up the steps and into the shadowy alcove leading to the big red front door. The child was her world and she would do anything to keep it whole.

****

Lissa stepped into the marble-floored atrium of the Liberty building in downtown Gaithersburg and entered the waiting elevator. She checked her reflection in the elevator's mirrored ceiling and adjusted her angled bangs that fell haphazardly across her forehead. She liked the new look her stylist gave her, but it was hard to get it to stay nice. The muted *ping* of the elevator signaled its arrival, and she took a deep breath before exiting. She swept into her workspace, flipped on the computer, and peeked above the cubicle wall into her boss's office. His balding head shone in the desk lamp. She let out the air she'd been holding, relieved he hadn't noticed her lateness.

A check of her inbox revealed several junk mail notices and, fortunately, nothing important pending. As she went through general office tasks—typing a memo, filing a truckload of reports, and ordering the monthly office supplies—the butterflies in her stomach wouldn't quit; the date with Brian kept her buzzed with anticipation.

During the departmental meeting, she glanced at the clock, counting the minutes until she could leave. It was nearly quarter past eleven and her boss droned on. She sent up a silent prayer the meeting wouldn't go over and glanced at the clock again. The time dragged. Only two minutes passed. She needed to be on the road in ten minutes. *A watched clock doesn't tick, is that it?* Like a watched pot never boils. Okay, she'd ignore the clock. Her palms now moist, she wiped them on her skirt. *Tick, tick, tick,* she was aware of the time on the clock but tried to stem her obsession of having to check every other second. Instead of checking every few seconds, she played a game of trying to guess what time it was and vowed not to look until at least a minute had gone by. Eleven twenty-one…eleven twenty-two? She snuck another peek at the clock. Eleven twenty-seven. She'd wanted to leave by eleven twenty-five. Already late, a wave of anxiety swept through as she bolted out of her seat and made a beeline for the elevator.

****

Stuck behind a bus puffing out gray exhaust fumes, Lissa held her breath as long as she could to keep from inhaling the acrid odor that managed to seep into the car. Who knew how many carcinogens she'd inhaled over the years? Now that she was conscious of the dangers, she avoided them as best she could. Running late, the traffic in front of her managed to slow down to a turtle's pace. Apparently, this was a phenomenon in rural towns as well as big cities. Lissa tried to merge into the faster moving lane but without any luck. A big utility vehicle sat in the lane next to her chugging a putrid scent of diesel fuel. She bit her lip. *Oh, brother, come on.* Her insides twirled nervously like a ball of yarn slowly unraveling.

The last time she saw Brian was fifteen years ago,

and only briefly at the impromptu meeting outside of his house the day her college friend Deb Atkins took her to Pinewood during spring break. He carried a hefty weight back then and she pictured what he might look like now. Still a towhead? Gained more pounds? It didn't matter, really. Her feelings for him overrode anything external. The serendipity of him walking up the sidewalk to his house just as they drove down his street left her glowing. "*Maybe, we'll see each other in another decade or two*," had been just her clever throwaway line for conversation's sake. Who knew those words would actually come true?

By seven minutes to noon, Lissa turned onto Battalion Street. She still had a few minutes to find the restaurant. Another three blocks down stood the train station, and she was relieved seeing The Train Stop restaurant next door.

She pulled into the parking lot and spotted a decent spot farther down by the bus depot. Nervous perspiration gathered under her arms. She grabbed a tissue and blotted up the excess moisture and then peered into the rearview mirror to study her face. Her skin looked fairly clear except for one blemish in the middle of her forehead. She cringed at how makeup didn't quite cover it perfectly with the moisture from the humidity now slipping the makeup off. She rummaged through her makeup kit for the beige concealer and reapplied the smooth liquid in layers, patting it in place with her ring finger. *Gray hair and acne. How lucky could a girl get?* After checking her face again, she swooshed on a layer of rose lipstick, blotted it with a fresh tissue, and stepped out of the car with a minute to spare.

A few people gathered on the station platform adjacent to the restaurant. A teenage boy wearing a backpack lingered by the tracks; he stood a little too close for comfort, and Lissa thought about pulling him back by one of the straps. Today, people would think that too intrusive or worse, some kind of an attack. She dismissed the notion. An elderly woman sat perch-like on a bench with her hand resting on a black cane, and two twenty-somethings huddled together—one of them apparently dishing something humorous amid the other's high-pitched squeals of laughter.

Turning toward the restaurant adjacent to the station, she wondered if Brian were already inside. She hated waiting—for anything. *Is he coming or am I going to be stood up?* She paced ten steps and then turned around to pace back. A heavy metal scent permeated the platform, and the marina blue sky was quickly paling to white. Oddly, something wasn't right, and Lissa had the surreal sense of someone watching her. Was Brian in the restaurant checking her out ahead of time? She turned around and continued pacing. Then in the distance, a male figure in a dark suit came walking from the opposite end of the tracks. *Is that him? It must be.* Her heart went from a nervous fluttering to a thumping overdrive. As the figure got closer, his face broke into a broad smile. *Brian.*

"Hey," she called and raised her hand in a girly wave. *Wow, he cleans up well. Nice suit.*

"Look at you," Brian replied and swept her into his arms.

The moment she heard his voice, the coil inside her slowly unwound and the tension eased.

"You look great," he said, charming her with his

perfect smile and sparkling blue eyes.

"You, too," she gushed. "It's so good to see you after all these years."

His sandy hair grayed a bit at the temples, and though some creases sprouted around his eyes, his boyish handsomeness still shone through. He'd lost his baby fat and dressed in his sharp clothes, he resembled a high-end suit model. His woodsy cologne, intoxicating.

In the buttery yellow light of the cozy restaurant, Brian and Lissa settled into a corner booth in the caboose room of the train-themed eatery. Between the clanging of silverware and the piped-in jazz music, along with the other patron's voices bouncing off the hardwood floors, she wished for a more private location to hear his soft-spoken voice. The boisterous women two tables down drowned him out. Certainly, she wanted him all to herself.

"I'll admit I've been stalking your Facebook page," Lissa said with a shy smile. *What would he think of her now?* She quickly blurted, "Your wife and kids are beautiful."

He curled his lips up modestly. "Yeah, the girls take after Angie, that's for sure."

"Where did you meet her?"

"At work."

"Nice," she said, nodding. "Lovely family. You're blessed." Lissa's heart dropped a bit. She knew there was a chance he was married but still held out the hope that he wasn't. *Okay, no harm done. He's a great guy...no wonder he's married.*

Brian placed his elbows on the table and folded his hands together as though about to pray. "Yeah, about that," he began. He looked down and then at her. "Unfortunately, my wife and I are having some problems right now."

"Oh?" she said, shocked at his announcement. "That's too bad." Though she was sorry for his situation and sympathized with him, deep down there was a part of her that remained ambivalent. For a moment she had a strange inkling of pleasure. Inappropriate, for sure, but was it wrong to feel a tiny bit—glad? If their marriage problems couldn't be resolved or were too difficult to overcome, he'd be a free man. How does one control her heart?

Brian set his lips in a firm line as though resigned to whatever it was. "Ah, it's life. Our issues have been going on for some time now. Seems like Madison is the most affected, my step-daughter."

"How old is she?" Lissa asked. His Facebook pictures painted an entirely different life than what he shared now.

"Seventeen. My wife was married before we met. Her husband ran out on them. I felt so bad for her, for both of them," he said, twisting the gold ring on his third finger around with his thumb. "And then after a few dates…well, we became an instant family not long after that."

Lissa nodded politely and in the back of her mind wondered whether she would have had a chance with him if she hadn't moved away. Junior high? High school? If she'd stayed in Maryland, who knows? He'd always been special to her as far back as third grade. Call it a crush, but whatever it was, he was in his own league. A fleeting thought of kissing him went through her head.

"Angie's child was such a sweet kid in the beginning," he continued. "But now—stubborn, headstrong. Scares me sometimes." He shook his head helplessly.

"There's another girl, too?" Lissa asked, remembering the pictures.

"Yes, Heather," he said. "She's eight."

"Eight? Oh, that's how old my Lacy is. Small world." She brightened for a moment and then shook her head, mirroring him. "The teen years are tough, but I'm sure Madison will grow out of it."

"Juvenile Hall should help," came his sober reply.

"She's been to Juvenile Hall?"

"Not yet, but I've threatened her with it." He balled his fists. "If you only knew the trouble she's caused."

The waitress approached the table and served plates of antipasto, goat cheese salads, grilled chicken breast sandwiches, and café lattes. As they reconnected, Lissa didn't dare ask what Brian's step-daughter did to make her a potential candidate for Juvenile Hall. She only knew one boy, Jimmy "Hot Rod" Stuart, from her old Bryn Mawr neighborhood, who went there. Never a girl. Of all the people to have a wayward child, Brian Pickering, the smartest and most upstanding kid in grade school, was the last person she could imagine having a child that needed professional counseling. Sometimes, things did not make sense.

"I'm sorry, Bri," she said, hoping her response sounded genuine and not saccharin.

He shrugged. "Not much I can do that I haven't tried already."

"More coffee, sir?" the waitress chirped, hovering over the table, holding the carafe.

36

Brian moved his cup closer. "That's good, thanks," he said, raising his hand. Lissa politely shook her head and held her hand over her cup. "I'm good, thanks."

Brian reached for the sugar packets, keeping his focus on her. "So enough about me, how about you, Liss?" His eyes danced, and her stomach did a little leap at the magnetic charge bouncing all around her.

"Oh, my daughter and I are doing fine—just trying to adjust to the change—you know, new friends, new home, that kind of thing." She paused. "And, I'm…I'm single now." Blood flushed her cheeks at the mention of her marital status, hoping he didn't think she implied anything. Of course, he couldn't read her mind and wasn't even aware she had a crush on him since grade school. Can a school crush still linger after all these years? She hoped soft lighting would help to hide the flush in her cheeks—and the stupid blemish in the middle of her forehead. "My husband Jason," she continued. "He died—in Afghanistan." Brian leaned forward and nodded sympathetically. "His third tour of duty." *Tour of duty? Sounded more recreational than laying one's life on the line kind of work.* This was the first time she spoke of it without getting a knot in her stomach. The liberation so freeing, she continued. "I begged him not to go, but…" She shrugged. "But you *men*," she said, injecting her words with light admonishment to all the male species. "You can be so headstrong, right?" She gave him a half-smile as she pictured Brian and Jason together. Same age. Similar handsome looks. Would they have been friends, she wondered?

As she spoke, Brian kept his eyes on her and seemed to be hanging on her every word. Her heart lightened when he reached across the table and put his hand on hers. A jolt of electricity coursed through her veins. *Whoa, what was that?* Her whole body warmed to his touch.

"So where are you living now?" he asked as she recovered from the unexpected response to his touch. Smooth skin, clean nails. His hands were prettier than some women's.

"Well, um, we moved into the second floor of a Victorian on Bellevue Avenue. The flashiest house on the street—a gray clapboard with pink shutters."

He winced mockingly. "*Pink* shutters?"

"I know. Flamingo pink. Can't miss 'em." She grinned.

"Didn't you used to live around there?"

She nodded. "Yep, right by the park. I loved that place. I plan to send my daughter to camp there this year. If I can afford it, that is."

They continued chatting for over an hour, sharing the good old glory days and all their mutual history. Lissa erupted in laughter at his anecdotes and he, too, at hers. Each story as memorable as the next brought out a lightness she hadn't felt in a long time.

"Remember the clubhouse?" Lissa asked, taking a sip of latte.

He nodded. "You were the only girl," he said with a grin. "How could I forget?" He held her gaze. Electricity soared through her again, and she looked down, embarrassed by her warm feelings.

"Do you need to get back to work?" she asked when he casually glanced at his watch, taking it as a signal the date was over.

He shook his head. "Not really."

What does that mean... he wants to linger? "I'm sure the chief of security has something on his work plate," she said coyly. She casually picked through the remains of grilled chicken—though, at this point, she wasn't the least bit hungry.

"Yes, but," he flashed his trademark smile, "I know how to delegate."

Another tiny shiver shot up her spine. Their lunch date did not begin with any romantic intentions. At least, not on her part. But now—? Her heart leaped at the thought of something more. Was something brewing between them? Brian's story being true, she wondered about his motivations for initiating the get-together. Did he like her in *that* way? A tingle of excitement ran through her at the possibility and she studied him further to get a read on his body language. If he did like her romantically, he was keeping his feelings to himself. Understandably. He'd always been a quiet kid in school and nothing much ruffled him as it did the other children. Mature and reserved beyond his years.

Except today, one thing gave him away. The twinkling in his eyes. Every time she spoke, his gaze lingered on her as though he were soaking in her every syllable, every inch of her, and she couldn't deny the warm feeling he gave her. Sparks flew each time he flashed his toothpaste ad smile and from the looks of things, she sensed he had his own sparks simmering somewhere below the surface.

Brian held the door open for her, and she stepped outside. The afternoon sunlight played on her face and shoulders in a light caress, and the world appeared crisp and startling in clarity as though she saw the station, the tracks, and everything around her for the first time. A sense of anticipation hung in the air. *Was she in love?*

Brian faced her. "This has been nice, Lissa."

Her heart sang with anticipation. This was more than a reconnecting date. The air of new love swept in and practically lifted her off her feet. "It has, Bri." She gazed into his eyes. "Thanks so much for lunch."

"My pleasure," he said and gave her a smile.

At the moment she leaned close to kiss him, the restaurant door directly behind her flew open. A young woman rushed out and knocked right into them, leaving Lissa nowhere to fall other than right into Brian's arms.

"Sheesh," she said, "What's her problem?" *Was she crying? Dumped by a boyfriend?*

Brian glanced over her shoulder at the retreating figure. A funny look came over his face. Then without a word, he planted a kiss on her cheek.

"We'll have to do this again sometime," he murmured; his soft voice sending a quiver down her spine.

She melted. "Sounds good. Maybe we will."

They stood face-to-face as the rumble of the incoming train shook the platform. Their amiable small talk came easily right from the moment they met, and she longed to stay with him for the rest of the day, wishing he didn't have to go.

The power of the train's engine was no match for the pistons churning inside her own heart. The strength of her heartbeat at that moment could rival any source of electricity—even a locomotive engine.

Chapter Six

Lissa's body still tingled as she made her way toward the parking lot. Before reaching her car, she stopped. She forgot to pick up a souvenir from the restaurant. No matter what, she wanted to remember this lunch date. She turned around and went back inside. In the dim foyer, a large glass bowl filled with red matchbooks sat on a corner table next to a dish of mints. She plucked one out.

Back in the car, she turned the key to the ignition and a whiny, scratching sound usurped the familiar purr of the engine. She tried a second time to start the car. And a third. No response. *Great.* Helpless to how an engine worked, she didn't know what to do. She'd had AAA towing service for years. Jason insisted on it. Though now, the membership had expired.

After another unsuccessful attempt at getting the car started, she banged her hands on the wheel in frustration. *Dear God, please...* She said a quick prayer and thought about who might be available to give her a ride at this time of day. She first thought of Brian, who never really left her mind after he boarded the train. His well-cut suit, the way he rolled up his cuffs, his clean-cut face flashed in her mind. If she called him, would he come running to help her? The damsel in distress. She laughed to herself at her wild imaginings. He was probably still on the train. She hadn't made many friends at work, and no one she knew lived out in the rural sticks of Pinewood. Miss Rucker? No, the woman didn't drive.

A bus pulled out of the depot, leaving it empty except for a lone taxi. "Okay, Lord, it's just you and me here," she said aloud and popped the lever to release the car hood. At the front of the car, she felt around for the little latch under the hood and cringed as her fingers rubbed up against the greasy interior. She fiddled around helplessly trying to locate it.

"Come on," she said, still searching until it seemed a futile exercise in frustration. "This is ridiculous."

She went back inside and grabbed a spare napkin tucked into the console. With her hands relatively clean, she reached inside her purse for her cell phone. "Oh, great," she said with a sigh. Not finding it, she thought back to earlier that morning and quickly realized it was probably still on her desk. Anxious to get out of the office to make it to the restaurant on time, she absentmindedly left without it. She fumbled for change to make a call, hoping to locate the rare pay phone that had become scarce these days. With a handful of quarters in hand, she stepped out of the car and headed toward the depot.

"Need some help, ma'am?" a voice called out. The man, wearing a baseball cap, looked familiar, but she couldn't quite place him.

"My car won't start," she said, relieved to find help so quickly. *Thank you, Lord.*

"That's too bad. Let's see here if I can help ya. That your car over there, the green one?" he asked, pointing behind her.

"Yes, the Toyota," she said with a nod.

"Okay, can ya pop the hood for me?"

"Sure." *Better you than me.* She got back inside and reached for the release knob.

"Once more," he shouted. "Okay, got it." He propped open the hood of her aging car and rooted around the engine. She hoped he knew what he was doing. Well-intentioned men had come to her aid before, but their efforts proved useless because the car needed a professional mechanic with the necessary parts to install. This guy, with his pulled-down cap and southern drawl, reminded her of Gomer Pyle.

He called out, "Okay, now try to start her again."

Her? Ugh, she hated when anyone referred to an inanimate object as a female. Cars, boats, hurricanes. *Why were they always female?*

She turned the key. The car coughed. Then she turned it again and the car sputtered and then revved to life.

Thank you, Lord.

He closed the hood and came around to the window.

"How do I thank you?" she asked, amazed at the good fortune.

"Aw, wasn't hard," he said, dusting off his hands. "Sometimes, the electrical contacts get stuck is all."

"Thank you so much. I really appreciate your help." She wanted to reach out and hug the guy.

He tipped his cap. "Glad to do it."

The man stood for a moment oddly transfixed as though he were lost in thought, and Lissa was so sure she knew him—but from where?

"I'd like to pay you," she said, reaching for her purse. She dug inside and pulled out a five-dollar bill.

"Here, this is for your effort."

"No, no. You don't need to pay me." He palmed both hands toward her, shooing the money away.

Lissa waved the bill, prompting him to hold up his hands in mock surrender.

"No, no, I don't want your money," he said with an aw-shucks sheepishness. One of his front teeth was missing. His boyish expression coupled with the gaping hole brought her back for a moment. Then the realization hit her. Two feet away from her stood her old schoolmate, Donny McCall.

"Donny?"

The man's head perked up.

"I'm Lissa Leeds—from school." She smiled.

He pointed his finger at her and grinned. "Lissa Leeds."

"Donny, you haven't changed much at all." *Except for the missing tooth.*

"I can't believe it," he said, beaming. "I thought I saw you around town. I wasn't sure at first."

"Yep, I just moved back to town this past winter."

He shoved his hands inside his back pockets while maintaining his jack-o-lantern-like grin. "So what brings you back here?"

"Work, mainly. And I've always loved Pinewood."

"Never left myself. I know this town like the back of my hand," he said, glancing back at the cab stand. "Drive a cab now." He gestured toward the depot with his thumb. "And a little photography," he said, lifting his chin. She nodded appropriately.

Lissa and Donny chatted, sharing anecdotes about growing up here until she suddenly became aware of the time; she couldn't believe it was past three. Lacy's camp would be letting out soon. Even if she left this very second, she would be late.

"Listen, sorry to run," she blurted, hating to interrupt him, "but I need to pick up my daughter. But, hey, let's catch up. I'm on Facebook. Why don't you friend me? It's Lissa Leads Logan." She prattled on. "But I'm single now."

She wanted to kick herself for mentioning she was single. *Why do I keep doing that?* She imagined him knocking on her door for a date. The former square dance partner turned dinner-and-a-movie date. *Just her luck.* "A lotta L's there, huh?" He chuckled, rubbing the back of his neck.

"Tell me about it," she said with a smile and tossed a queen's wave as she pulled out of the parking lot.

Chapter Seven

In an effort to save time, Lissa made a last-minute decision to take a shortcut to avoid the heart of downtown traffic. Lacy expected her to arrive at the designated time of a quarter after three, and Lissa was seldom late. She held her breath, hoping to make it through the lights—pressing her foot on the accelerator at every yellow-turned-red light, which was technically orange. Any cop waiting to send his siren blaring would have a fair reason to ticket her, but she hoped that by God's grace, she'd go unnoticed.

Lissa's luck soon ran out as she managed to get caught in red lights the rest of the way. A wave of guilt pressed in. If she hadn't spent so long at lunch with Brian, she would have already arrived at Lacy's school. The image of his sky-blue eyes gazing at her and his shy smile lingered in her head, giving her a rush. Of course, the car not starting was the likely reason, she tried to assuage herself. It would have given her trouble anyway and taken up just as much time, possibly even more, if she hadn't run into someone to help. The fortuitous run-in with Donny McCall was a godsend.

She unconsciously pressed her lips into a firm line, trying not to look at the clock on the dashboard. The LED light displaying the time only brought more anxiety. Better to not know than to fight time. She already knew it wasn't on her side. Why add to the stress? Her back muscles clenched tight as a coil.

Twenty minutes later and very late, she pulled into the main entrance to Lacy's school where Lacy stood, teary-eyed, alongside her teacher beside the pond, holding her hand. Her child's broken spirit sent her own to fracturing. *Poor kid.*

"So sorry," Lissa called out the window as the car skidded to an abrupt stop.

"Oh, we understand, Mrs. Logan," Nan Westbrook said respectfully. Her arm still hung around Lacy's shoulder. "I told Lacy not to panic. We knew it wouldn't be long before you'd get here."

Lissa got out of the car and walked around to where they stood. She bent down and wiped away a strand of stray hair clinging to her daughter's flushed cheek and wrapped her arms around her. "I'm sorry, baby, traffic was a nightmare."

"Told you, Lace, your mom was just stuck in traffic," her teacher said as she squeezed Lacy's shoulder.

"Thank you so much, Ms. Westbrook, for helping her," Lissa said, appreciatively. She opened the back door of the car, and Lacy climbed inside.

"Not a problem, Mrs. Logan." She turned to Lacy. "And we'll see you tomorrow, right? Can you give me five?" She leaned into the car holding her hand out. Lacy brightened and raised her hand to mirror Nan's. "And we'll be making some neat stuff in art," she said, her eyes widening.

The inkling of a smile crept onto Lacy's lips, which delighted Lissa.

"Bye," Lissa said with a wave and shut Lacy's door before getting behind the wheel.

"Honey, you okay?" Lissa glanced in the rearview mirror after she pulled onto the main roadway. Lacy seemed unusually quiet compared to her normally loquacious self. With no reply from her daughter, Lissa reached back to squeeze her daughter's knee. Understanding her only child was beset with a fear of abandonment, most likely, an inherited trait. *"It's part of being Italian,"* her Aunt Celia once said about the worrywarts in the family.

Lissa would do anything to help her daughter overcome this debilitating characteristic. Her memory drew back to her own crisis when she was a little girl. Tears came easy for her as well at eight years old, the time she lost her mother in a department store. Lissa stole another glance at Lacy curled up in the corner of the back seat. This would not be the time to preach but she felt compelled to say something. Finding the balance between mother and friend could be tricky at this age, so Lissa tread cautiously.

"Lace, I'm sorry. I know exactly how you feel, honey," she began. "I've been in your shoes." She waited to let her words sink in, hoping Lacy would come around. "But remember, God is watching over us, right? I will always be your mother and here for you, you know that but when I'm—" She stopped, not wanting to paint too harsh a picture. "What I mean is that Mommy depends on God and…well, he's the only one we can truly rely on." Lissa knew this concept hadn't hit home for her daughter yet, though she hoped one day it would. Reading her daughter Bible stories and talking about Jesus was how Lissa shared her faith with her daughter. Spreading the seeds was all she could do for now. She knew her only job was to sow;

God's job was to reap.

"Hey, idea. Do you want to see the house where Mommy grew up?"

"I guess," she said without much enthusiasm.

"It's not far, you'll see," she said with an extra brightness to her voice, hoping to encourage her daughter back to her usual spritely self. She made a turn and headed toward the main artery through town.

So many memories flooded back as she drove through the downtown part of the city. She pictured the streets as she once knew them.

"This is surreal," she gushed as they passed St. Jerome's Catholic Church and Jimmy John's Sandwiches. "I remember that place... aww, it's still there," she said, catching a glimpse of the Baskin-Robbins ice cream shop, recalling the sticky-hot summer days when her mother gave her change to buy a cone, which she ate right on the curb, the hot sun in her eyes.

"Keep an eye out for Queen's Chapel Road. That's where my old house was," she said, feeling a happy flutter in her stomach. "I think it's coming up soon if I have my bearings right." She looked back at Lacy who moved from her curled up position and was now sitting erect and looking out the window. "Queen's Chapel Road...sounds like something out of a fairytale, doesn't it, honey?"

"Uh huh," Lacy replied. A trace of lightness in her voice.

They passed Jefferson Street, Prince Rainier Avenue, and then King's Court Boulevard. "Yep, there it is, just beyond those trees on the right. Twenty-four-twelve. It should be coming up soon—at the top of the hill." A huge oak tree marked a fork in the road. The engine ground as the car strained to make the steep incline. "There, there it is, Lace." She pointed excitedly like a school girl.

Lissa pulled up to a red-brick two-story colonial with black shutters. The quiet neighborhood murmured with the delicate sounds of chirping birds, and the air held the sweetness after a freshly fallen rain. Lissa gazed at the property tucked in among the shadow of surrounding trees and overgrown foliage. A nostalgic tug pulled in her heart. She disappeared into the moment, remembering her carefree days of childhood—her mother hanging laundry...planting daffodil bulbs in the front yard...sitting on the front steps with her best friend Ruthann Lowry as they sucked fresh watermelon and swatted the bees away.

"There's a park right down the street. At least, there used to be. It's probably a housing development or a golf course by now."

Lissa drove around Pinewood, first taking in the scenery of Glen Meadows Park. The winding narrow road led through rolling hills where sterling vistas Lissa knew from childhood appeared new. In the hollow at the bottom of the first hill, a set of train tracks cut through some overgrown vegetation. The once vibrant steel devolved into strips of rusted metal atop loose shreds of timber. Lissa mentally relived carefree days when she hopped along the trestles and stepped up on the smooth metal rails pretending it was a balance beam.

"I used to hang out down there," she said, pointing to the tracks, "with some of the neighborhood kids. We thought it would be neat to put a penny on the rail before the train came by to squash it, but I was afraid the coin would make the train somehow slip off its track. "Goofy right? Lissa made a silly face, mocking herself hoping the moment drew Lacy out of her funk.

Lissa glanced over the hills. "Oh, look, honey," she said, pointing out the window. "There's a kissing bridge."

"*Kissing bridge*? Why do they call it that?"

"They're historic bridges from back in the nineteenth century. There was a legend in town about them. Apparently, they said that in Pinewood, more people fell in love there than in any other town in Maryland after they'd driven over one, and wherever Cupid's arrow fell, the kindling it stirred would simmer forever."

The landscape, bathed in variegated colorations and altered with time, vaguely resembled the version she knew from back then. Lissa marveled at the beauty of the park's ambiance and the changes that evolved over the decades.

"Now, I'm going to show you where I went to school."

****

Perched high above a circular driveway, Lissa's former elementary school, Chillum Acres, looked abandoned. The long red-brick building that once sat formidably upon the hill appeared diminutive now with patches of wood splayed across the windows.

"Oh, no. Is it closed?" Lissa's heart sank.

The old school, once modeled in the likeness of a mighty frigate, had turned into a lifeless relic docked for repairs in the shadow of its heyday. The huge flagpole in the center of the circular driveway standing at attention without Old Glory looked naked. She pictured Brian gathering the red, white, and blue material from the thick white cords with one of the other kids in class who'd been assigned to flag duty with him. The image of his bright blond hair and marina blue checked shirt lent a nostalgic rush to the otherwise somber scene.

"Too sad. I didn't expect this." She gazed up at the school. "I loved this place—everything about it… the teachers, my classmates…" Her voice trailed. A wistful feeling came over her at the remembrance of it all. She bubbled with an overwhelming desire to go inside, but with Lacy along for the ride, she thought better of it.

On the way home, Lissa checked on her daughter once more. "Love you, Lace," she said and stole a glimpse of her through the rearview mirror.

"Love you, too, Mom."

Finally. Her little girl was back to her normal, sweet self.

Just then, something piqued Lissa's curiosity. The car traveling directly behind them looked familiar. She thought she saw it earlier before she turned into the school. The imposing SUV looked expensive. There weren't too many of those around town. *Was it following them? How long had it been there? The white van from Bryn Mawr popped into her head.*

Lissa's instinct kicked in, and she tried to keep her imagination from running away with itself. *Calm down, Lissa. It's not the same vehicle. Relax. It might be white, but it's not a van.* She shuddered to think her worst nightmare in Bryn Mawr had followed them to Pinewood. Then she realized, no. The van driver had been a rumor. People's imaginations getting the best of

Beyond the Roses

them. It didn't take long for Lissa's imagination to rear itself. She took a deep breath and tried to settle down her out-of-control thoughts. There could be any number of reasons for what appeared to be a tailing car. This was a direct route that could have led to just about any major artery. *It's just a coincidence,* she told herself. There are lots of people with places to go, things to do. *Why be paranoid?* The person behind the wheel—a man or a woman—she couldn't be sure. Was the driver headed to Rockville? Or Hyattstown? Lissa's mind spun with possible scenarios until the implausibility of them shook her to her senses. She whispered a quick, panicky prayer.

At the upcoming roundabout for Constitution Avenue from Michigan Street, she made a left. The car continued to follow. While this might be just a coincidental happenstance with any plausible explanation, only one haunted her—the worst-case scenario: Years ago, her mother told her about her own similar predicament—the day she was followed by someone unknown.

Lissa fought to disguise her fear from Lacy and didn't say a word, hoping not to telegraph her worry, though her pulse raced as she zigzagged through town with the stranger in clear pursuit. Whenever she turned, the car behind did as well. *What is this person doing?* Her heart thrummed. She didn't want to drive directly home—then the person would know where she lived. She didn't know what to do. She scanned the sidewalks. There were people walking along the street oblivious to her situation. She wanted to reach out and alert the man who just stepped into the street to cross. *Help me*, she said with her eyes, hoping he'd notice her desperation.

But how could anyone help her now?

Up ahead, she saw a police car. The tension in her stomach eased when the black and white vehicle pulled up to a large gray building and parked in front of the marble steps leading to—*a police station. Thank God.* She quickly pulled to the curb directly behind the police car. Two officers got out and one glanced Lissa's way.

"Everything okay, ma'am?" asked the tall, well-built officer who eyed her curiously.

She turned around. The SUV was no longer in sight.

"Yes, Officer. Everything is okay," she said, forcing a smile.

"You sure, ma'am?"

"Yes. Yes, we're fine."

Fine…for now.

Chapter Eight

Lissa turned off the shower. The gray and white tiled bathroom billowed with steam. She wiped down the foggy mirror with a tissue, and before she could inspect her face, a fuzzy reflection met her when the steam rolled right back. *Just as well.* In the partial clarity of the reflection, she could imagine herself without wrinkles. She wasn't sure when time began to etch marks into her once porcelain skin, particularly her eyes, where fine lines now feathered like tiny fans at the outer corners. Probably too many summers out on the beach in South Jersey. She made a silent vow to start wearing sun block. After slipping into her shorts and tank top, she went to the window to let in some air and clear the steam.

She lifted the shade and her breath caught. She stifled a scream seeing a dark-haired man standing at the window. Miss Rucker didn't mention any men living on the property. An icy fear ran through her. *Was he the person in the SUV?* He looked to be at least her age, if not older.

"Hello, there," he called through the window. He lifted the wrench and waved it in the manner of a white flag in surrender mode. "I'm here to fix the air conditioner, ma'am." Her initial fear simmered to a keen curiosity and she lifted the window open a few inches. "I wasn't aware it was broken," she replied, flatly.

"Just maintenance, really. Landlady wanted to make sure her tenants are taken care of."

"Really?" she replied, eyeing him. *Landlady? Didn't he know her name?* He looked a little too clean to be a maintenance worker. His fingernails weren't smudged with dirt and the leather tool belt around his waist seemed brand new, along with his denim overalls.

"Live two doors down. I don't think we've officially met. I'm Mike Hempstead."

Okay, so he says he's a neighbor—still doesn't get him off the hook. The question: 'Do you drive an SUV?' popped into her head but she thought better to squelch it.

"Lissa Logan," she said, her guard still up.

He nodded his head in a gentlemanly fashion. "Welcome. Pleased to meet you, Miss or is it Mrs. Logan?"

"I'm a widow," she replied, wondering why he needed to get so personal. Her guard, already high, shifted her nerves into third gear.

His eyebrows furrowed. "Um, sorry 'bout that." His hazel eyes glinted, and she was glad she dressed before raising the shade.

"Well, don't let me keep you from your work," she said, somewhat relieved that he wasn't a Peeping Tom, though she still had reservations. Anyone can put on a tool belt or overalls and claim to be a repairman.

He gave her polite nod before she closed the sash, locked it, and pulled down the shade.

Chapter Nine

Lissa pulled the last of the clean laundry out of the dryer as her phone rang.

"Hello?"

"Hey, it's me," came the familiar southern twang.

"Robin, it's so good to hear from you," she said and threw the towel she'd been folding back into the basket and plopped down on the sofa.

"Just wanted to say hi and see how y'all were doing."

For all of her fears about the car stalker and the man by the window, hearing Robin's voice gave her comfort.

"Um, we're all right," Lissa answered with a feigned lightness. She didn't want to dump her imaginary problems onto her friend, particularly on a long-distance call. She'd painted Pinewood so perfectly to Robin. *Never even heard a police siren.* Her words came back to haunt her in light of her recent encounters. She didn't have the heart to tell Robin she'd already spoken to the police. She cleared her throat. "So how about you?" she asked, her tone upbeat.

"Oh, we're all right, but we sure miss you."

"Aw, goes the same for us, too," she gushed as she reached into the basket for a towel and began folding the laundry.

"Alex still talks about Lacy."

"That's so sweet, Robin. So, how 'bout you guys? What's going on?"

"We're making progress. I picked up two more children to sit for—a pair of twins."

"Excellent news. Glad to hear it," Lissa replied, cheerily.

"So how's *your* work?"

"Well, work is work, right?" Lissa forced a chuckle. "Actually, Dr. Billing is great. He lets me work from home a couple of days a week."

"That's awesome."

"I know. Such a blessing."

"Good for you. You deserve it. How's the new school working out for Lacy?"

"I haven't heard any complaints yet, so I believe she's adjusting. She's made some friends and has a new best friend. Becca.

"Wonderful. And the romance front?"

"The *what* front?" Lissa laughed. "I don't think I know that territory." Not wanting to jinx her new relationship, she kept it to herself, though she was bursting to share the good news.

"You have got to be kiddin' me, Lissa Logan. Any man would be glad to have you on his arm."

"Oh, Robin. Spoken like a true friend."

"I'm serious, woman. You're the whole package."

"Not."

"Stop. You're ridiculous is what you are. You'll see."

Bursting to tell her, Lissa couldn't hold in her secret much longer. "To be perfectly frank," she began. "I *am* seeing someone."

"Get out. Who?"

"Just an old friend."

"Friends are good, right?"

"The best." A smile drew to her lips.

"So don't keep me in suspense, woman. Tell me."

"His name is Brian." She tried not to sound like a school girl.

"*Brian*," she echoed. "I like it."

"Turns out, I've known him practically my whole life. We went to grade school together. Smartest kid in the class." She beamed.

"Are you serious about him?"

"Well…" Lissa replied, her voice raised an octave. Then she quickly lowered it. "He's married."

"Aw, shoot. Oh, well."

"At least, for *now* he's married."

"Oh?"

"Technically. Seems there's trouble there. He's unhappy. His wife is, too. She's probably been unfaithful. He didn't come right out and say it, but the clues are there."

"Oh, boy. Poor fella."

"I know." She paused. "I'm in a quandary, though."

"How so?"

"Well, he's still married. I don't want to hold my heart out to a married man. Yet I can't help myself."

"Have you…?" Robin let her words drop.

"Oh, no! You mean—"

"You know." Robin interjected.

"Robin, you know me better than that. I could never sleep with him." She paused, knowing how much she wanted to—oh, yes—but then thought of the example it would set for Lacy. "We've just met a couple of times, you know. Getting our feet wet, I guess."

"Honey, I know you wouldn't do that. Of course not. You're pure as the driven snow, girl, but you know how persuasive men can be."

Women, too, she thought, knowing the manipulations of her own impulsive heart. With God, she was able to put her thoughts into perspective. Sometimes extra-marital sex without the benefit of marriage can lead to nothing but heartbreak, she knew. It was everywhere, and she wanted no part of it. With everything in her life now, stability was the only thing she wanted. For herself—and Lacy. There was no room in her life for a broken heart—at least, not from casual sex. No way.

"Well, listen, sweetie, I don't want to keep you from anything," Robin interjected in her usual self-deference.

"No, no, you're fine. I'm just waiting for Lacy. She'll be home any minute now. She's out with the dog, so I'm just hanging out, folding some laundry."

"You got a dog?"

"No, no, it's not ours," she said with a chuckle. "It's the landlady's."

"I didn't think you'd have one."

"You know me well, Robin," she said, a smile in her voice. "Dog hair, doggie-doo, shots... no thanks."

Robin cackled on the other end. "It's true. Dogs are a lot of work," she added. "But I'm not laughing at you, hon," Robin said through her laughter. "I just pictured you with one is all."

Lissa folded the last towel and noticed the light at the window had darkened. *Was it twilight already?*

"Hey, Robin, listen, I need to run. I think I hear Lacy. Can I call you back later?"

"Oh, sure, honey, not a problem."

"Thanks. Talk to you soon."

Chapter Ten

Lissa's insides tingled when Brian spoke her name, especially over the phone. Every time he called, she had the same reaction; his voice wrapped around her heart. She pressed the phone to her ear, vicariously picturing his whole being standing next to her, and didn't know how much longer she could be attracted to a married man. It was killing her. Whenever he called or offered to come over, she struggled with her desire to move their relationship forward. How long could she be just friends with this guy?

"Hey, Brian," she said in her silkiest voice, feeling sexy just saying his name.

"What's doing?" he murmured.

"Not much, just finishing up a report for work. And you?"

He blew a breath into the phone. "I'm pretty sure it's over."

Lissa's spirits deflated fast. *Us? We haven't even begun.* "W—what do you mean, Bri?"

"I just moved out."

The abrupt impact hit hard but in a good way. *Seriously? Out of your house...like you're separated?* Lissa's heart went into overdrive. "You did?" she inquired calmly. She wanted to do a back flip.

****

Parcels of farmland the color of wheat and sage sat

like oversized postage stamps in the sprawling countryside at the foot of the purple-gray Appalachian foothills. Wavy clouds of heat hovered over the roadway in the near distance.

"I could gaze at those mountains all day," Lissa said, dreamily, of the majestic scenery as Brian drove I-340 toward Farmington Heights on the other side of the county. "With this gorgeous scenery, it's no wonder they wanted to live in the country." She looked at him. "You nervous?" she said with a chuckle and nudged his thigh.

He glanced at her and then fixed his eyes back on the road. "Who, me?"

"Yes, you," she said and playfully knocked his arm. "Meeting my aunt and uncle is the same as meeting my Mom and Dad. They would have loved you." She patted his knee. "Aunt Celia is my mother's only sister, so she's pretty special to me."

The hint of a smile grew on his lips. "Nope, not affected in the least."

She saw through his pretend demeanor. "Liar," she said softly.

He reached for her hand and laced his fingers in hers. "Well, maybe a little."

"They're the salt of the earth, and I've been telling them about you." She paused. "Actually, Aunt Celia remembers you from when we were kids, so you're not like a stranger or anything."

"Do they know about my marriage situation?"

"No, I haven't exactly told them that part of your life," she said. "I don't think they'd shine much to know I was dating a married man."

"*Technically*, married, Liss. My wife's been

unfaithful, and we're separated. I don't think that constitutes a marriage." He eyed her. "Do you?" He squeezed her hand tighter for emphasis.

Lissa smiled, elated at his words, though she knew men sometimes liked to play the field under the guise of being *separated.* "I guess not," she demurred. *Hope he means it.* She looked back at Lacy who was in her own little world as she stared out the window.

"Honey, I don't think you remember Uncle Charlie and Aunt Celia, do you?"

"Yeah, I do," she replied as though her mother should know better.

"You *do*?"

"I remember him from when we were watching cartoons at Nanny's house—in Philadelphia. I remember because he laughed out loud, and I always wondered what was so funny."

"Oh, okay," Lissa said. "I'm glad." Her mind flew back to the times he'd get mad at her for touching his electronic components—"*Don't touch it"*—he always managed to say before she got within arm's length. Or his car—same thing. He hated fingerprints on his car.

The roadside sign read three miles to Farmington Heights.

"Looks like we're almost there," Brian said.

Lissa combed a hand through her matted waves and refreshed her lipstick.

****

"Hi, Uncle Charlie," Lissa called out the open window while waving as Brian turned into the driveway of the tiny salt box. Charlie wore a short-sleeved madras cotton shirt with khaki shorts and was holding a chamois cloth to the hood of his shiny black Mercedes.

The home, set in the fifty-five-plus community on a rectangular-shaped parcel, bore creamy yellow siding amid similar houses on the street in complementary colors of pale blue, buff, and eggshell white. Still a strikingly handsome man at seventy-something, Charlie had a bright smile and a full head of wavy silver hair.

"M'lissa Marie." A broad grin lit up his face as they approached. "You're gettin' prettier ev'ry time we see ya." He dropped the chamois into the bucket and stretched his burly arms around her as Lissa gave him a quick kiss on the cheek. "And little Lacy…you look just like your momma, sweetie."

Lissa glanced around the well-tended property. "Your grounds look immaculate, Uncle Charlie. Love the garden. The roses are gorgeous."

The floribunda and tea roses bloomed in a riot of pink, yellow and scarlet, coupled with clusters of baby's breath and other petite florals.

"Yep, they're Celia's baby. She's been tending them for years."

Their inviting fragrance drew Lacy, who stood over one of the bushes inhaling the blooms. Lissa pulled out her Coolpix camera and snapped a picture of her in mid-sniff.

"Well, don't just stand out there, c'mon in." Aunt Celia's mellifluous yet no-nonsense tone rang out from the doorway. A tuft of silver curls spilled out from under her powder blue head scarf, and the flowery blue and yellow tunic she wore billowed as she waved them inside.

Lissa hastened to the door to greet her. The scent of freshly washed linen permeated the air as they embraced.

"Well, looky you. You haven't changed much at all, my sweet M'lissa." She grinned ear-to-ear and then spotted Lacy. "And look at that sweet one. Could be your twin when you were a youngin'." She bent down as Lacy approached the step where she stood and threw open her arms. Her eyes misted as though she were moved at the very touch of the child. She wiped her eyes and announced, "I've made lunch and a fresh batch of cookies. C'mon in."

****

"More cookies, anyone?" Celia held out a cookie tin lined with waxed paper.

Lissa held up her hand, "None for me, thanks. I think I've already gained weight just sitting here." She patted her hip and glanced at Brian, who gave her a wink.

Celia mock frowned. "Oh, you're perfect, Lissa. You look like a teenager."

"Aw, thanks, Aunt Celia." Lissa glanced at Lacy, who leaned over her plate, picking up the crumbs one at a time. To Celia: "I think she liked them."

"There's plenty more," Celia said.

"She's had four already. That's sufficient—"

"But, Mom," Lacy interjected. She held up her index finger. "Just one more?"

"Okay, Lacy. Just one more. But just once I'd like you to finish your peas like you did those cookies."

"They're so small, Cel," Charlie said, holding up one of his wife's homemade butter shortbreads. "Why don't'cha make 'em man sized? These look like buttons." He then shoveled a couple of cookies into his mouth at once. Some of the powdered sugar, unbeknownst to him, fell onto his chin.

With a hand on her hip, she said, "You're gonna choke on that, Charlie." A moment later, he let out a cough. "See? Drink some coffee before that dough lodges in your throat."

"They're so good, right, Uncle Charlie?" Lissa chimed in as her uncle took a sip of coffee. He raised his head and nodded as he clutched his breastbone. She picked up a broken section of a scone on the serving plate and popped it into her mouth.

Celia pursed her lips at him in mock jest and picked up the coffee urn. "More coffee, Brian...Lissa?"

"Oh, no, Aunt Celia, but thanks," Lissa replied.

"I'm good, too." Brian held up his hand. "Everything was great, Mrs. Rossi."

Mrs. Rossi? It sounded so formal to Lissa. Maybe one day, he'd exchange the *Mrs.* for *Aunt.*

Lissa got up from the table and moved into the adjacent living room. On the coffee table lay an assortment of magazines, including several copies of AARP and a stack of National Geographic. Beside them lay a thick leather-bound book with gold embossed pages. She sat down on the sofa and picked up the book.

"That's an old photo album I brought out from storage. I thought you might enjoy it," Celia said from the table.

"May I help you clear the table?" Brian asked Celia, who pooh-poohed the idea.

"No, no, Brian, but you're a dear to ask. The dishes can wait."

"There are some pictures of you in there, and your parents, too." Charlie added through a mouthful of shortbread.

Lissa opened the album. Lacy plopped the last bit of cookie into her mouth and left the table to join her. "Here I am, Lacy," Lissa said, pointing. "That's me with my mom and dad, and here we are at the house where I grew up." Before turning the page, she looked over at Brian, who still lingered at the table making small talk with Uncle Charlie. "Come join us, Bri." She patted the spot next to her where she sat on the sofa as he approached. His thigh brushed hers as he seated himself. Her daughter on one side and her boyfriend on the other. *Perfect.*

"And here's a picture of us at Ocean City. Oh, I remember that day."

"Is that your mother's sister?" Brian asked.

"Yep, Aunt Lydia." She nodded and pointed to the man in the picture. "And that's Uncle Joe."

The picture was taken near the beach where the water appeared to rise ominously above their heads as the waves crashed behind them.

Lacy pointed to the picture. "That water looks scary."

"It does, doesn't it? But it's just an optical illusion, honey." Lissa replied.

"Yeah, but it looks like the water is about to come up over their heads."

"Sure does, very scary," Brian said with a wink to Lissa, and then he turned to grab Lacy by the shoulders as though pouncing like the waves.

"Hey." She giggled, basking in his attention.

Lissa grinned and slapped his knee affectionately.

In the back of the album, some papers tucked in the binder—a Yuletide prayer, a recipe for banana walnut bread, and some faded newspaper clippings including one of a strange looking man. Lissa studied it curiously. "Who's this?"

"Oh, that," began Celia, "it's one of your Dad's cases."

"Is that Hellinger?" Charlie asked, reaching for another cookie. "Biggest case we ever saw in Pinewood," he added. "Drug cartel busted to smithereens."

A bald-headed man with a mustache stared from the faded news clipping. Something about him looked familiar. Lissa quickly scanned the story.

The First Federal Bank of Pinewood noticed things weren't adding up... the county's sheriff's department was called in to question a money laundering sting in operation for two years, conducting deals all over the US, and sending money across the world. Over $2.4 million was added to their coffers, and no arrests were ever made until a Mexican cocaine-trafficking cartel used accounts at First Federal to hide money and invest illegal drug-trade proceeds in U.S. racehorses, the FBI said...

Lissa's expression turned serious. "Hmmm...I never knew this."

"What's the matter, Mom?"

"This guy," she said, tapping the edge of the album with her finger. "He looks so familiar."

"It's Joe Hellinger," Charlie said. "He lived right here in Pinewood. His kids grew up here...probably went to your school, Lissa."

Lissa mulled over where she'd seen him. *The paper boy's father?* "Oh, yeah, I remember that kid. He went to the parochial school and delivered the evening paper—Robbie Hellinger. This was his father?" She paused. "Bri, do you remember him?"

Brian studied the photo. "Not sure," he said and slowly shook his head. "But vaguely, I recall the story about him."

"Do they still live around here?" Lissa asked.

Charlie wiped his mouth. "I don't know for sure. Do they, Cel?"

Celia pursed her lips. "I'm sure the father is still in prison, right?" She looked at Charlie.

"Sure hope so," he said, pushing away from the table.

"But as far as I know, they're still here. His kids and maybe even his grandkids," she said.

"Yep. Locked up for a long time." Charlie slapped his hands together and rubbed them quickly. "Thanks to your daddy, M'lissa."

Puzzled, Lissa didn't remember any of the details. As far as she was concerned, Pinewood was just a sleepy little hollow where nothing bad ever happened. No particular distinction ever hailed from the small community. Rumors of the Hellinger family's hate for her father never passed by her ears. Her mother made sure of it. Then a year later in 1978, her father died in a car crash—an accident her mother believed was orchestrated on purpose, though the police never found anyone to blame. That was something she wondered about for a long time. Now, her curiosity about it rose again.

Lissa shut the photo album as distant memories stirred of Pinewood, her family—and the Hellingers.

Chapter Eleven

The sun hovered low in the distant arms of tree branches like a ripe blood orange. The atmosphere, still. From the second-floor landing of the old Victorian, Lissa took in the expansive view of the neighborhood. The steeple of St. Jerome's church pierced the clear sky to the north, and to the south, the silo of Runnemede Farms. Lissa checked her phone. The time was 5:45 p.m. Lacy was usually home from walking the dog within fifteen minutes—twenty at the latest. She was at least ten minutes late by her calculations. As a single mother, she kept a close tab on her daughter just like her own mother had. Ever since the day Lacy left the house without a word, Lissa's anxiety kicked into overdrive. Like her Aunt Celia once said... the *worry* gene ran in the family. Lacy had been an angel the first six years of her life, but once she entered school, her independent spirit took flight—and Lissa's panicky nature right along with it.

As the cars streamed by, her heart beat faster when a white vehicle passed; images of the white van back home in Bryn Mawr and the SUV that tailed her here in Pinewood haunted Lissa way too often. She had to stop being so anxious but wasn't sure how. *It's just a car. Somebody has to drive them. But was it the same one?* As much as she tried to talk herself out of being paranoid, she still couldn't let go of the old memories that had turned her world upside down. Like a suspense movie where it's hard to pull away from looking, she watched the cars pass on the street below, hoping not to catch sight of anything else big—or white.

She paced back and forth on the landing; with every step, the floorboards squeaked under her footsteps. The rhythm distracted her, and she made a game of trying to pace without making a sound. Blinking lights near the bushes caught her attention. The yellow-green neon glow of lightning bugs gave her a source of giddy delight as a child, especially the potent joy of capturing one of the tiny creatures in her palms. The hunt for them at the precise moment—just past twilight and before the shadows of dusk—after an afternoon of playing in the pool became the capstone of her summer days. Now, the neon lights failed to conjure the same light-hearted delight and only underscored her daughter's lateness. Not even warm thoughts of Brian could tear her heart away. Not right now.

Lissa continued to pace as she waited for Lacy. She mentally drew back to her own dog walking experience when, at ten years old, she took care of Mrs. Elmore's two Scottish terriers, Baird and Laird. Such sweet, quiet dogs. She was happy her daughter was following in her footsteps and taking on some responsibility at an even earlier age.

She leaned on the handrail, resting her forearms on the rough wood. While fiddling with her phone, her elbow slipped, and the phone dropped from her hand onto the floorboards. In a flash, it bounced and then slipped between the rails and fell two stories before landing on the macadam driveway below. The loud crack when it shattered sent a ripple of regret through her. "Oh, no," she cried and ran down the stairs to retrieve it. *Great. Another expense.*

****

Lacy yanked on Toby's leash in frustration to keep him moving. The dog kept stopping every few feet to sniff out something only a dog could find interesting. The scent of wet earth filtered the air, and a swarm of tiny gnats floated above her head. This part of the forest smelled awful. Like a dirty washcloth. She curled her nose with disdain.

"How much longer?" she called. "Are we almost there?"

"Almost," the boy yelled back to her from up ahead.

She could barely see him at this point. Eventually, the forest gave way to an open space, and he ran in the direction of an old gnarled tree. Beside it lay a tattered wooden trunk.

"Here it is." He pointed at the old heap with tarnished brass hinges.

"What's in it?"

His eyes lit up. "Treasure."

"What kind?"

"I don't know yet but it's heavy, so there has to be something valuable inside." He pulled the trunk a few feet and then stopped. "Help me carry it," he ordered.

Lacy, ready to oblige, grabbed onto the rusty handle with one hand while Tommy took the front and led the way out of the woods. The dog gave another low growl. They stopped and started a few times, struggling to balance the unwieldy weight. By the time they reached the swim club, the handle started to burn her palm, and she dropped her end of the chest.

Teetering on the edge of the newfound discovery, she asked, "Are you going to open it now?"

"No, not yet."

"Why don't you open it? Don't you want to see what's inside?" she coaxed.

"It's locked. I'm taking it home. My brother will know how to open it." Tommy rubbed his hands together and then wiped them on his jeans, not sounding the least interested in sharing the treasure.

Before they picked up the trunk again, out of the corner of her eye, Lacy spotted someone else in the woods—a man wearing a white T-shirt and a red baseball cap. He stood at the edge of the clearing adjusting what looked like a large telescope.

"Quiet, Toby," Lacy instructed and lifted her finger to her lips. She wondered why the dog suddenly became agitated. *Was he upset by the stranger?* In the midst of Toby's barking, the man turned around and looked at her.

"C'mon," Tommy said, picking up his end of the trunk. "Let's go."

The man gave her a wink and turned back to the telescope.

Lacy thought she heard the sound of her mother's voice in the distance. She cocked her ear. "That's my mom...I gotta go." She jerked Toby's leash, announcing, "Come on, boy," and darted across the swim club's parking lot for home.

****

In the near distance, Lissa heard the sound of a barking dog. At the corner, the familiar beige-and-white-spotted Toby appeared. At the other end of his leash, her daughter. The idea of scolding Lacy for being late flitted through her head—she'd been here before—and then she thought better of the message it would send. No, she would not punish her little girl for her own imaginative worries. She simply breathed easily once more.

"Hey, Mom," Lacy shouted, spotting her mother who waved from the landing. "Guess what? We found something."

"You did?" Lissa matched her daughter's enthusiasm. The child could have told her anything, and she would have responded the same.

"Yeah, me and Tommy."

Her brow tightened. "Who's Tommy?"

"He lives up the street," she said, signaling behind her.

"Okay, well, drop off Toby with Miss Rucker and then you can tell me all about it later. We're going out for dinner tonight."

****

A little after six o'clock, the warm scent of seared meat permeated the entryway of the cafeteria style steakhouse at the Prince George's Plaza shopping mall. Standing in line with their trays, Lissa checked out the hot entrees available—veal almandine, broiled flounder with lemon sauce, pasta alfredo. Lacy followed behind, incessantly chattering about her earlier adventure in the woods.

"It definitely had something inside, Mom," Lacy gushed.

Lissa nodded encouragingly as she moved up the aisle. "Sounds exciting."

"It was. It's like we were on a treasure hunt."

Lissa eyed the roast beef. "Looks pretty rare." She

pointed to the carving station where large slabs of reddish-pink meat were warming under a heat lamp. "Just the way you like it, Lace."

Lacy's eyes grew large. "I love it when it's pink in the middle."

"I think I'll get some, too," she said as she caught the eye of the chef and pointed to the beef. He cut several thin slices for each of them. "Thank you," she said, taking the plate from him and then moving her tray down the buffet line. Sticking with her new low-carb diet, she skipped the desserts, trying not to even catch a glimpse of the sweet confections on display.

Lissa paid the cashier for their meals and they headed for a table in the corner by the fireplace.

"Mom, it was so neat," she exclaimed, sticking her knife and fork into the juicy meat.

"I know, you told me." Lissa unfolded a napkin and placed it on her lap. "That's exciting, sweetheart," she said with a forced nod, wondering how long Lacy would remain on the topic of treasure.

"I wanted him to open it, but it had a lock on it."

Lissa took a sip of ice water. "So who is this Tommy person again?"

"He's from the neighborhood," Lacy replied, scooping up the baked potato.

"Does he have any brothers or sisters?"

"An older brother."

"How old is he?"

She shrugged and answered through a mouthful. "I don't know how old his brother is, but he drives."

"I meant your friend Tommy. How old is he?"

"He's way older than me, Mom." She swallowed. "Oh?"

"Yeah, he's in the fifth grade. I think he's like ten or something."

Amused at her daughter's perspective, Lissa smiled to herself and struggled to refrain from laughing. "Yes, that *is* old."

When they finished their meals, they left the restaurant and strolled around the mall, eyeing the mannequins in the window of the Girl Scout shop.

"I like that one, Mom." Lacy pointed to a mannequin wearing a Brownie uniform. "That's the kind of beanie I want."

Lissa once graciously accepted a hand-me-down Brownie uniform from a lady at work whose daughter, now a Girl Scout, no longer needed it. The outfit just about matched the newer ones with the exception of the beanie that appeared lighter in color than the traditional chocolate brown. The day Lissa brought the outfit home and placed it on Lacy's bedroom cedar chest to surprise her, she took one look at the beanie and cringed, claiming it looked just like *peanut butter.*

"We'll see," was all Lissa could offer at the moment. As the sole breadwinner, she still hadn't assessed her discretionary expenditures in light of the move. "When I can see my way clear, honey," she said, hoping that would soon end the conversation. Right now, she needed more important things like a new cell phone. "Let's see if they have a phone store in this mall, Lace." Lissa led the way to the middle of the first floor of the huge plaza and perused the directory posted by a small fountain surrounded by greenery. "Here it is," she said and took Lacy by the hand to go check out what they offered.

Stepping out of the mall with her new purchase in

hand, a light rain fell as they headed for the car. While pulling out of the lot, Lissa checked her surroundings for anything unusual. The image of the imposing SUV still lingered in her head, a vivid reminder of how swiftly potential danger could arise. Lissa remained vigilant—and worried. Though the incident occurred over a month ago, the memory was still alive.

Once out of the lot and on the main drag through town, she tensed at the first set of headlights in the rearview mirror. Even an innocuously driven car that happened by coincidence to be traveling in her same direction gave her pause. The vehicle maintained a steady pace behind her at some point after she left the mall. She couldn't tell the make or model through the drizzling rain, nor could she tell whether a man or a woman was behind the wheel. After the next busy intersection at Queenstown Boulevard, she looked into the mirror again and saw no one behind her. She breathed out a sigh.

"We don't have an umbrella," she said to Lacy as she pulled into the driveway. She turned off the engine. "So we'll have to run." She gathered her purse and plastic bag containing the new phone. "Okay, ready? Let's go."

She made a fast exit from the car and dashed up the steps with Lacy close behind. Once at the top, the overhang above the door shielded them from the ongoing downpour. The feature was one of the things Lissa admired in the old Victorian. She rummaged for the key and inserted it into the lock. When the door opened easily, she froze.

"We can't go in," she said tersely. Lissa quickly grabbed Lacy's arm and fled back down the steps.

Chapter Twelve

A policeman stood imposingly at the front door, his big, bulky frame filling the doorway. Embarrassed to be seen in her nightshirt by a total stranger, Lissa gathered the lapels and fastened them with her arms folded across her chest.

"Hello, Officer," she said.

The policeman tipped his head. "Just wanted to come by again, make sure everything was all right."

Still nervous from the incident only hours before, she slowly pulled the door open. The police escort back into their apartment earlier had given her courage to walk inside, though barely loosening the tension in her emotional belt but a notch. Hardly enough to feel at home.

"Yes, I think we're fine." She cast a glance back toward the bedrooms.

"Need me to do another run through, I'd be happy to do so."

She closed her arms tighter across her chest. "I think we're good."

Earlier, the burly cop had clunked through the rooms—the jarring sight of his pistol and leather holster gave her a mild shock—and shone a flashlight inside each of them, under the beds and the closets. Finding nothing amiss, he made some notations in a notebook and left. A thick scent of musk and leather trailed behind him long after his investigation was over. Ironically, his very presence upset the delicate balance of house and home almost as much as the earlier intruder.

Later, Lissa looked up from her dressing table to see Lacy standing at the doorway.

"Mom, I can't sleep."

The sight of Lacy in her pink pajamas and bare feet as she held her pillow sent a ripple of empathy through her.

"Don't worry, honey," Lissa assuaged her daughter. "The burglar, or whoever it was, is gone."

"But I don't want to sleep alone."

"I know, honey, come here." She held out her arms and Lacy snuggled into her. "I know it's scary. I'm scared, too."

Even after a thorough search by the police, her thoughts whirled of possible places where the intruder could still be hiding. She could not shake the fear of knowing a stranger had crept into their living space—and could still be there. Somewhere. Was he still inside, hiding somewhere the police didn't check? She once heard the story of a man who slipped into the narrowest of places and held his breath to escape notice. How hard would it be to sneak behind her one of her winter coats or even inside one of the garment bags? Lissa's mind raced with possible scenarios.

"The police searched everywhere, honey. They checked all the rooms. There's nothing to be afraid of now," she said, emphasizing her assurance. "You may sleep here tonight," she said, pulling back the sheet and comforter. With that, Lacy hopped onto the bed and Lissa tucked her in. "But just tonight, okay?" Lacy's green eyes stared up at her from the pillow.

Lacy didn't seem completely convinced, but Lissa held out hope that Lacy understood and trusted her.

As she undressed for bed, thoughts of Brian came to mind again. She desperately wanted to call him. The sound of his deep voice was just the salve she needed right now—a balm for her frazzled nerves. A security officer himself, of sorts, for the Department of Defense, he'd be the one to help allay her fears. She wondered what he was doing tonight. An abrupt knock interrupted her thoughts. In her robe and slippers, she went to the door.

"Everything all right, Ms. Logan?" Miss Rucker asked, her face pinched with concern. Her gaze shot past Lissa into the apartment as though there was something just beyond she should know about.

"Oh, Miss Rucker, come in." Lissa parted the door wide and ushered her inside.

"I saw the police and didn't know what the matter was," she said, hurriedly. "What happened?"

"Not to worry," Lissa said and patted the diminutive woman's stooped shoulders to confirm things were under control. As nervous as she was herself, it felt good to at least maintain a sense of composure. "Everything's okay, *now*."

"Now? What happened, dear?" She nervously cast a glance around the room.

"We had a break-in. When we got back home from dinner, I found the door unlocked."

"Oh, my, you don't say." She clutched her chest.

"Yes, so I was afraid to go in. We immediately ran down to the car for safety where I called the police on my cell."

"Anything stolen?"

"That's the strange part." Lissa glanced around. "I don't know for sure. I really can't say."

"Oh, I'm so sorry to hear this. Really, I am. You should have come to my door. I feel terrible." Miss Rucker raised both hands to her head as though wanting to squeeze her brain.

"It's not your fault," Lissa said.

She nodded. "Yes, yes, I'm afraid it is."

"Why, Miss Rucker?" Lissa asked, disbelieving.

"I never warned you."

"Warned me about what?"

"The Peeping Tom."

"There's a Peeping Tom?" Lissa's voice rose.

"I thought it was just my imagination at first. I'm getting old, but I'm not too old to notice things. I've heard he hangs out in the woods in the park," she said, gesturing. "He carries around a—oh, whad'ya call 'em? Those things to spy with."

"Binoculars?"

"No, no, a big thing." She shook her head. "Anyway—"

"When did you first notice him?"

Silence.

"Miss Rucker?"

She seemed hesitant to answer.

"When did you first notice that there was a Peeping Tom?"

"I'm not sure really when he began, but I noticed a strange man lingering around the neighborhood around the time you and your little girl moved in."

Chapter Thirteen

Pop! Lissa awoke from sleep with a startle. The sound came from somewhere inside or outside the house, she couldn't tell. Her limbs froze as she strained to figure out where or what it was. Maybe it was a newspaper landing on her doorstep? She didn't sign up for a delivery, though sometimes freebies were distributed. The narrow stairway leading to the second-floor landing was a long shot. Who'd have that good an aim?

When the Freeze King refrigerator erupted with a loud burst by day, she reasoned the appliance had seen better days and was presently on its last leg. Come the wee hours, the same sound rose more threateningly and making the connection was not as easy. Any pop or even the click of the heating/AC unit outside the window evoked a sense of danger in her vivid imaginings. *Was it the refrigerator? A rock at the window?* The perils of the night lent even the innocuous sounds of the unknown an ominous foreboding.

The clock read eight minutes after six. Gray light appeared around the outer edges of the window blinds. Lissa braced herself under the bed clothes and her mind continued to whirl with possibilities. She knew the sound wasn't loud enough to be a gunshot but what was it?

She got up. At the bedroom doorway, she paused.

Gentle water droplets pattering on the windowpanes usually relaxed her, but now, standing stiffly at the threshold to her bedroom, her rigid body defied every drop. She waited for a brief minute listening to the water sluice through the gutter in metallic plinks. *Just rain or maybe a loose tree limb finally snapped and fell.* Satisfied that whatever it was had passed, she padded back to her bed. Before she hopped back in, the sound came again. She stopped short. The sound didn't come from the direction of the window. It sounded like the creaking of wooden floorboards. The outside stairway. Was someone on the landing?

Lissa hesitated before moving toward the front of the apartment, simultaneously attracted and repelled by whatever stood beyond the doorway. Her heart thumped as she tiptoed toward the door. Maybe it was Miss Rucker who needed help, or Mrs. Houser, who shared the other half of the Victorian's second floor. She braced against the door frame and stood on her toes to peer through the peephole, careful not to stumble or bump into the door and hoping the old floorboards wouldn't give away her presence by creaking.

The misty light of daybreak revealed something on the landing. Leaning against the corner of the railing lay a single pink rose.

****

"Hey, Robin, it's me."

"Hey, sweetie, everything okay?"

"It's just so odd." Lissa stared at the wilted rose.

"What's going on?"

"This flower…on my doorstep." She ran her thumb and index finger along the velvety petals.

"Someone send you flowers?" Robin's voice lilted.

"Just one. A pink rose."

"What's wrong with it…stem broken?"

"No, it's beautiful. But sometime last night or this morning, who knows, it was just sitting outside the door by the railing. But there's no note or anything."

"Hmmm…, well, *red* would be romantic. And yellow is friendship. I guess pink is somewhere in between," she drawled, cheerily.

"I asked Miss Rucker about it, like if she noticed anyone out of the ordinary come by, but—"

"Hey, maybe it's from Brian?"

Deep down she hoped the rose was from him, but if it was, why didn't he leave a note or card with it? No, something was odd about it.

"I thought to call him but then—oh, I don't know," she said, feeling a strange uncertainty.

"You'll never know unless you ask him. Just call him, Liss."

She caressed one of the petals feeling the smooth, velvety texture. The light citrus scent was her favorite. *How did he know she loved the smell of citrus? She never told him. No, this wasn't from Brian.*

Chapter Fourteen

"She said there's been a Peeping Tom in the neighborhood," Lissa explained to Brian, cradling the phone to her ear. "And it's all kind of materializing now."

"What, exactly?" he asked, his voice mixed with concern and curiosity.

"This creepiness." Lissa peeked out between the blinds at the living room window. "It started in my landlady's living room the day I signed the lease agreement. It wasn't what she said but how she acted—or reacted—to something she saw in the window or heard outside, I don't know. But when I asked her, she was mum about it. Then when the break-in occurred, she seemed so guilty of something. Like she knew who did it."

"What did she say?"

"She just warned me that there was a Peeping Tom in the area. I always thought they were harmless...too timid to do anything but look."

Lissa remembered the report of one on Ingraham Street back in the 70s. She heard her mother and another woman talking about it. In the course of the conversation, Lissa picked up words like *Peeping Tom* and *harmless* both in the same sentence.

"They could be harmless, but then again..." His voice trailed and then turned serious. "So what about the break-in? Anything stolen?"

"That's something else that's weird. The police searched everywhere. There's nothing missing and nothing out of place." An uneasy feeling swept in again.

"It's good you reported it to the police. Now there's a record."

"I'm just thinking about what my landlady said about the Peeping Tom." She paused. "She made it sound like it could be one in the same person."

"Strange. Is she sure?"

"I don't know," Lissa replied, her paranoia rising like a bad dream.

"At least nothing was stolen, Liss. And you and Lacy are *safe*."

Although Brian underscored their safety, his words didn't make a dent in her still raw, helpless feelings. Red flags waved. "Yeah... but—"

"Don't get yourself all worked up over this. Just have the lock changed. Get a deadbolt or a chain, something more secure. Insist to the landlady—um... Miss what's her name? Miss Tucker—Trucker?"

"Rucker," Lissa offered.

"Whatever. Have her do it immediately. Make sure to put a chair or something under the doorknob before you go to bed tonight."

"I will."

"Oh, and Liss." He paused. "I can come over tonight if you want me to."

His words settled over her like a summer shower. Lissa's heart soared. *Come over...tonight*? "Oh, Brian, that's so sweet of you, really."

"So...you want me..."

Oh, yes. If you only knew how much.

"…to come over?"

As much as she did want to see him, she didn't feel it appropriate.

"I'd love for you to come over, Bri, but maybe not tonight." She wanted to kick herself, but she knew in her heart of hearts that it would be better to wait. "I'll be okay…really."

"Well, how about later today. Can we meet for coffee…say in an hour?"

She glanced at the clock. "Oh, sure, that would be fine."

"Our spot, okay?" he murmured.

"Sounds perfect," she cooed. "I'll meet you there."

When she hung up with Brian, her thoughts raced. With everything on her mind, she forgot all about the rose. The pressing thoughts of the Peeping Tom usurped everything. She wondered what the intruder looked like and if he were young or old. She hoped the police would find him soon. A nagging question hung in her mind: *If he didn't come to steal anything, what did he come for?*

Chapter Fifteen

"So the rose wasn't from you?" Lissa held her breath waiting for Brian's reply.

"A rose?" he said curiously. "I—um, I haven't given anyone flowers in a long time." He signaled the waitress. "Not that I haven't thought about it," he said with a sheepish grin.

Embarrassed, she tried to save face. "I was just making sure. You know, had to check all my bases."

"Now maybe if it was your birthday, but that's not until May, right?" He spoke with a sensuality she hadn't heard before and uncrossed his arms. She delighted in the tingle running through her body. *He remembered.*

"Yes, May. The twenty-fourth." She felt giddy for a brief moment before the pressing urgency of the situation came into focus once more.

A waitress approached their table. "Hi, may I take your order?"

"Yes, uh, we'll have coffee—two coffees and..." he said and looked questioningly at Lissa. "You sure that's all you want, Liss?"

She nodded.

"You got it," the waitress said, grabbing the menus from the table before leaving.

He reached for her hand and pulled away the napkin she'd been fiddling with. "Hey, this thing really has you worried, huh?" His concerned eyes shone like crystal blue lake water in the afternoon sun.

"It's just so—so odd, is all. Plus that SUV stalker...and the guy at the window. I thought coming to Pinewood would be more...I don't know... peaceful." She shook her head in mock disgust. "Seems like it's one thing after the other."

A cloud came over his face. "Well, it looks like I'm going to have to look after you better." He winked. "And, it seems to me like you've got a secret admirer."

In her heart of hearts, Lissa hoped he was talking about himself. She shrugged coyly. "Do I?"

He reached for her hand. "Maybe more than one."

She melted at his touch.

"One is all I need," she said, staring into his eyes.

As they sat holding each other's hand, the strangeness of the pink rose still hovered like an unwelcome shadow in the back of her mind.

****

"Sergeant Matthews speaking."

Lissa cowered at the gruff, intimidating voice at the other end of the telephone.

"Hello—hello, Sergeant, this is Lissa Logan. You sent one of your officers to my house the other night?"

"Yeah, break-in. What about it? Someone break in again?" His voice boomed with testosterone. The sharp sound of gravel in his sonorous voice shook her for a moment until she realized it was just his defense.

"Yes, sir, well... I mean, no, no break-in—"

"You find something missing, ma'am?"

"Oh, no. That's not why I'm calling, sir. I wanted to ask you something. Now, it's not an emergency or anything, but something strange happened this morning."

"Go on," he barked.

"I just wanted you to know that I got flowers sometime after you left. Actually, just one flower. Someone left it on my back porch. And, well, other than being weird, I just wanted to report it. To get it on record."

"A flower?" His voice rose with perplexity as well as annoyance.

What was it with men and flowers?

"Okay, ma'am, I'll make a note of it," he replied, flatly.

"But I also want to report something my landlady told me—about a Peeping Tom in the neighborhood."

"Peeping Tom? In the park? Already know about it," he declared, gruffly.

"You do? Oh, good. So someone has reported it?"

"It's been checked out. Didn't find anything."

"Oh, okay, sir. Just wanted you to be aware of it. Thanks."

Lissa hung up the phone and stared at the flower, wondering whether to put it in water or throw it out.

Chapter Sixteen

"Calm down, honey. What happened?" She swept the hair away from Lacy's eyes and held her by the shoulders.

"This girl," she panted. "I was trying to pass and she—"

"Take a breath, Lace." Lissa studied her daughter for a moment. She seemed all right, except for the hyperventilation. She quickly went to the kitchen, grabbed a glass from the drain rack, and filled it with water from the tap. "Here," she said, handing the glass to Lacy. "Drink some water."

"This girl stopped me," Lacy said, taking the glass in both hands before chugging a gulp, "on the way home."

"Who was she?" Lissa's voice rose with concern.

Lacy, still panting, shook her head. "She had long dark hair and a red sweater...bigger than me. There was another girl there with blonde hair. I don't know them."

"Them? There was more than one girl?"

"Two." She took another gulp. "I think they're older."

"Just two girls?"

She nodded. "And Tommy's brother."

"Tommy?"

"You know him."

"The boy with the treasure?"

"Uh, huh. She also said something about our family."

"Oh?" Her curiosity rose. "What did she say?"

"She said we were troublemakers." She took another gulp.

"How does she know us?" Lissa asked, pointedly. She rested her hand on Lacy's shoulder for emphasis.

Lacy shrugged. "I don't remember," she said, before slurping down the rest of the liquid. "But she doesn't like us much."

Lissa didn't have a clue what the girl could have been talking about. *What trouble could I have caused? Unless the girl meant Daddy?* His only claim-to-fame in town was the Hellinger case. *Was this related somehow?*

Chapter Seventeen

"Hey, girl, it's been a while."

"Robin, I was just thinking about you. Glad you called." Lissa put the last of the dishes into the dishwasher, shut the door, and turned the dial on.

"Just wanted to check in."

"We're doing okay. And you?"

"Doing fine, thanks."

She moved to the living room and lay down on the sofa, glad to be off her feet.

"Are you still seeing Brian?" Robin drawled.

Just hearing his name made her into putty.

"Yeeesss," Lissa replied, giving the word two syllables.

"Is someone in love?" she asked with a smile in her voice.

"We'll see," Lissa replied cagily. "I don't kiss and tell, ha ha."

"Oh, girrrrl, I hope so. It's been a whole summer and now we're into fall...sounds good from this end."

"If it's meant to be, it'll be. All I can do is pray and wait."

"Yep, you got that right," Robin said. "So what else is going on?"

"Oh, not much. Lacy's invited to a party. Her first social affair. A girl from school invited her—Becca Robson, her current BFF."

"Now aren't we Logan girls running in prime social circles these days." Robin's voice lilted with light sarcasm.

"Why, yes, we *are*," she replied with a mock emphasis. "She'll be going as a ghost. I tried to talk her into being a head on a platter but—"

"Excuse me?"

"A *head*—on a *platter,*" Lissa explained, describing the do-it-yourself Halloween idea she once saw on an early morning kid's TV show where the costume featured a mock serving platter on a cardboard table designed to be worn on the shoulders.

Earlier that morning when describing the costume to Lacy, the child curled her nose. "Yuck. No way, Mom."

To that, Lissa asked, "So what do you want to be for Halloween?"

Lacy pushed a breath out of her mouth. "I don't know.

"What about a clown?"

Lacy shook her head.

"A hobo?"

"Nope."

Lissa rummaged in her bureau drawer and found an old black scarf that once belonged to her mother. "I know you don't want to be a witch." She put it back and continued searching for something appropriate. "So what if you just went without a costume?"

"Mom, the invitation says we're supposed to wear *costumes*."

Later, Lissa found an old white bed sheet, took a pair of scissors and a black marker, and went to work. Voila, a ghost costume. Without spending a dime. She hated everything about Halloween. She thought back to when the day used to be fun, but by age ten, the novelty had worn off. Lissa's phone indicated an incoming call. "Oh, Robin, it's Brian calling," she said, anxious with delight. "Talk later." She hung up and picked up his call. "Hi," she said warmly.

"Hi." His voice sounded sweet but leaden.

"Aw, you sound down, Bri," she said in a concerned tone.

"Naw, I'm fine."

"You sure?" she questioned, sympathetically.

He paused. "Actually, yeah, I am pretty down. Can you meet me somewhere?"

"Of course," she said, delighted at the invitation. "Our usual place?"

"Yeah."

"Okay, I'll be there in fifteen minutes."

****

Lissa stepped into the local café; the warm interior held a rich, espresso aroma. Brian sat in the same booth they normally shared. The diffused light from the glazed window cast his face in a warm glow, though after seeing his despondent expression, she wondered what was up. *Was he breaking off their relationship that was just getting started? Did he have cold feet?* A ripple of anxiety coursed through her loins.

"Hi," she said, sliding into the booth across from him. His expression opened up as she approached, giving her relief that this was not a verbal "Dear John" letter. "What's up, Bri? You sounded so sad on the phone."

She wanted to reach across the table and pull his thoughts out of his head. There was an air of mystery about him; there always had been: reserved, detached, unreadable. Yet she'd seen his warm side. He didn't show it often, but it was definitely there. Others she'd dated in the past had worn their hearts on their sleeves. Nothing turned her off faster than knowing a man's intentions immediately. Brian stored his in a vault—but kept the key handy.

His dour expression slowly softened. "I ordered your usual," he said.

"Chai tea latte with extra cream?" She smiled, happy he remembered how she liked her tea.

He nodded.

The waitress approached. "Chai latte," she chirped, "with extra cream?" She flashed a polite smile as she placed the tea on the table.

"Thank you," Lissa said, eagerly placing her palms around the steaming hot mug to warm her frozen hands. As she held the mug, she hoped he'd soon break the ice on what was on his mind. The latte would be so much sweeter if she could only relax. "Are you okay?" she asked, tentatively.

"Actually, I'm feeling a bit relieved." He lent a quick, taut grin.

Puzzled, she took a sip, careful not to burn her tongue.

He smoothed down the back of his neck with his hand and rubbed his temple. "I've been tired of swimming upstream."

Okay, he keeps talking in riddles. Maybe it's his way of delaying what he wants to say.

"I'm not sure what you mean." She pressed the mug to her lips to warm them.

He held his hands together on the table and looked

down. "There's only one thing that can come after a salmon swims upstream."

Fish? She pictured the silver-orange sleekness of migrating river salmon sluicing through the deep currents of cold water. After they spawn, they die. The thought hit her. *Was something in his life about to die? Was this his clever way... using imagery to poetically dump me?* Her heart sank.

The hot cup had turned warm and, in a few minutes, her tea would be cold. She held onto the mug to sustain the fading traces of warmth between her fingers as much as she needed to hold her own heart together from what Brian was about to unleash.

"I've asked Angie for a divorce."

His words made a beeline for her heart. The healing balm already at work. The tension in her abdomen fell away in a silent whoosh. Her heart soared and her imagination flew.

Lissa Pickering... Mrs. Brian Pickering... the names lit like a neon sign in her head before she had to tell herself to stop. She tried to remove herself from the thoughts peppering her head. Her supposing he'd ask her to marry him was premature, but it didn't stop her from thinking them. One part of her head said, "*Why wouldn't he? Soon he'd be a free man,*" and the other part said, "*Slow down, woman. Put the brakes on.*"

"Oh, Brian," she finally said once she got her mind in order. "The pain it must be causing you and your family. I'm sure it's unsettling to say the least."

He leaned forward and shrugged. "I think I'll be all right," he said, settling his eyes on hers. "In due time."

A moment later, something shifted under the table. The touch of his legs gently wrapping around hers. The heat was unmistakable.

Chapter Eighteen

In the still of the early evening, some trick-or-treaters made their way down the sidewalk. Among them, a little girl in a princess costume alongside an adult whom she recognized as Mike Hempstead. He waved from the sidewalk.

"Hi, Mike," she called from the open car window. "Nice weather for the kids."

"Sure is," he called back.

She slowed the car. "Hi, there," Lissa said to Mike's little girl who couldn't have been more than three. "I like your costume."

The cute child held up her bag. "My candy."

"Yes, I see. Don't eat it until Daddy and Mommy check it out first." He signaled his agreement by giving her the *thumbs up* sign as she waved and pulled away.

Traveling the main artery out of town, her mind flew to images of pins and razor blades and other sordid things people did to inflict harm on innocent children. Lissa wouldn't let Lacy eat anything that didn't go by her inspection first or accept anything from neighbors she didn't know. Her thoughts fell back to Mike, who outwardly seemed like a decent neighbor. His presence spooked her once when he was working outside her bathroom window, and she couldn't help thinking that anyone could pose as a repair man—the moniker just a convenient cover. *How many would-be-ne'er-do-wells pose as general contractors or maintenance repair guys*? Later, she realized it was just her own paranoia talking. Mike was a good guy and, apparently, an attentive, hands-on father as well. She turned on the radio, hoping to be distracted from her vivid imagination.

Trees morphed like chameleons out of their summer greenery into ripe shades of amber and crimson. Lissa loved this time of year. Though the trees were losing their leaves as winter dormancy loomed on the horizon, the showy display of electrified colors signaled the power of life within them. One last hurrah.

Becca Robson and her family lived on the other side of town in a well-to-do enclave of McMansions named *Golden Meadows Estates* in Elmdale. Lissa drove through the main entrance, admiring each of the houses—one just as ostentatiously huge as the next. She pulled up to 808 Larchmont Drive and parked in front of the Robsons' immaculate Tudor, the kind of house her mother would admire and say, "*I couldn't afford the front door."*

Floodlights the shape of tiny lanterns lined the stone walkway leading to the front door of the two-story stucco home and several more dotted the sprawling fieldstone borders. Lissa kept her eyes peeled on the black double doors graced with a cluster of fall-colored leaves and pine cones. A large spider web clung to the door frame; orange and black streamers hung from the trees. *How could anyone with a legal job afford such an immense house?* Becca's father had to be either a CEO or a drug dealer.

In the dim early evening light, she tuned the radio to a Christian station. A CeeCee Winans's song played.

Presently, a silver minivan idled in front of her and two children dressed as Spiderman and Darth Vader climbed inside. Another couple of children bounced down the Robsons' driveway—one wore a mouse costume and the other dressed as an elf. Behind them, a little ballerina came rushing past them and headed toward a gray Mercedes parked across the street. Some older trick-or-treaters sauntered along the sidewalk smothered in greasepaint and gothic clothing. *Good timing*, she thought.

Minutes ticked by. She glanced once again at the house. The stream of party goers dwindled and silence followed after the last of the vehicles pulled away. With her impatience rising, she fought the urge to get out and knock on the door, not wanting to embarrass her daughter by appearing too motherly.

A male figure came out of the Robsons' garage. Becca's father. She met him once along with Becca's mother at the school's first PTA meeting earlier in the month. They were older than most of the parents of grade school children and appeared closer to the age of grandparents.

Lissa turned off the engine and got out of the car. After surveying the well-heeled neighborhood from all angles, she decided to fetch her daughter who, more times than not, could easily overstay her welcome. Lissa proceeded toward the house.

"Mr. Robson," she called to him cheerily as he came down the driveway wheeling two large trash receptacles. "Hi, I'm Lissa Logan, Lacy's mother. How are you?"

Startled, he stopped short. "Oh, yes, hi. Please, do call me Jay."

"Oh, yes, of course. Lovely home you have." She raised her arm in a sweeping gesture toward the stately Tudor.

"Thank you," he replied, modestly dipping his head.

"I'm just here to pick up my daughter."

He cocked his head.

"Lacy…from the party," she offered.

"Hmmm." He lifted his hand to his chin. "Well, I think the party is over. In fact, my wife just told me to start cleaning up."

"You mean she's not still inside?" Lissa quickly cast her eyes over the man's property.

"I don't think so…now maybe I could be wrong."

Lissa's insides cinched and her thoughts scattered. "I dropped her off this afternoon around four and—"

"You know what?" he interjected. "She might just be using the bathroom or something. You know how little girls are," he added with a stiff chuckle. "Would you like to come in and wait?"

A wave of relief passed over her. *Of course.* She nodded. "Yes, could I?"

"Absolutely. I was just going to take these down to the curb," he said of the trash receptacles, "but they can wait." He made his way toward the house and beckoned her to follow. Jay led her into the garage and then through the door leading into the house. "Jan," he called out pleasantly from the kitchen while ushering Lissa inside.

The spacious hardwood floored kitchen was large enough to dance in. The cluttered table held the remains of what once had been a large vanilla sheet cake topped with chocolate icing, along with plastic liters of soda and fruit punch. Nearby, a trash container filled to overflowing revealed soiled paper plates, napkins, cups, and empty soda containers. Moments later, a tall grayish-haired woman appeared from around the corner.

"Honey, this is Lissa, Lacy's mother," he said, gentlemanly palming the back of her denim jacket.

Lissa lifted the corners of her lips and extended her hand. "Lovely to meet you, Mrs. Robson. I think we met once before—at school."

"Yes…yes, I do remember you," she replied with her own version of a polite barely-there smile.

Lissa cast a nervous glance around the room, hoping to catch a glimpse of her daughter or a note of her voice before announcing, "I'm here to pick up my daughter."

A flicker of uncertainty flashed in Jan's eyes. "Lacy?"

"Yes, I've been waiting outside but I decided it best to…" Lissa's words faded when she sensed her initial instincts come into play again. She mentally revisited dropping Lacy off in front of the pristine residence. The late afternoon light burnished the neighborhood in gold. She'd been awed by the lovely homes as they drove along the winding macadam. When they got to Becca's home, Lissa pulled up to the curb and watched her daughter get out and turn to go up the driveway, but did she actually see Lacy go inside? She couldn't remember. Exactly when she took her eyes away became a blur. She felt like a character in a Twilight Zone episode.

Jan lent a quizzical look to her and then to her husband. "Oh, I'm sorry," she said, shaking her head apologetically, "but I don't think any of Becca's friends are still here."

Lissa's knees started to tremble. Her worried expression must have given away her feelings as right then, the woman held up a finger. "But wait." She slowly stepped back, still signaling with her index finger to hold on as she retreated. "Let me check with Becca just to make sure. She's upstairs in her room. Lacy could be there, hold on a moment, would you?" She backed out of the room in what appeared to be slow motion.

With her whole body on edge, Lissa longed to follow her, or better, race right past the slow-moving woman who seemed to abide in a state of perpetual calm. Sometimes she wished to be the kind of person who exuded an unruffled grace instead of the tightly coiled state she often found herself.

Jay pulled out a tall hardback cane chair and pointed to it. "Please, sit down. May I get you something to eat or drink?"

Eat, now? People offered their hospitality at the most ridiculous times, she thought.

Jittery, she shook her head nervously back and forth like it was spring loaded. "Oh, no, that's okay, but thanks, I'll be all right." Her words came out fast and quivery.

She stood in the kitchen watching him clear the table. He shuffled back and forth to the sink and then ran the garbage disposal all while attempting to make polite small talk. She understood his need to put her at ease and admired his effort, but every word he said had little effect on her, and she went through the motions of conversation without really being present. *Was this man blind to the fact that her daughter could be missing*? The only thing on her mind was where was Lacy and why was this taking so long?

A strawberry blonde-haired child appeared from around the corner of the kitchen. "Hi, Mrs. Logan," the little girl offered weakly. The child stood diminutively next to her mother at the threshold. One look at their sober expressions and Lissa knew Lacy wasn't here.

"I'm afraid—" Jan began.

"Then where is she?" Lissa choked out. "Where could she be? She came to your house and now she's—she's gone?" She hated the rise in her voice. Not that it was impolite but that she had to raise it at all.

Jay reached for a paper cup on the table and moved swiftly to pour water and hand it to her in the manner of a peace offering.

"Where is she?" Lissa heard her voice as though it were disconnected from her body. The reality of the moment mirrored a scene from a Lifetime movie. This wasn't real.

"She left," the little girl said in a hushed voice.

"What?" Bile rose in her throat. "Left…when?"

"What do you mean, Becca?" her mother said, emotion rising in her voice. "When was this?"

Becca looked down at the floor. Her feet, dressed in fluffy pink socks, squirmed restlessly on the smooth hardwood floor. Silence.

"Becca?"

After another long pause, the child replied, "She left when we were playing pin the tail on the witch game."

"Why?" Jan asked, her curiosity mounting. "Why did she leave, Becca?"

Silence.

Lissa's insides bottomed out. Within seconds, she dropped the cup onto the table and ran out of the house. In the distance, she heard Mr. Robson calling after her. He'd been so calm and collected before but now there was urgency in his voice. In mid-stride, she kept going. No time for decorum now. She had to find her daughter.

Lissa looked up and down the street, straining to catch a glimpse of Lacy in the darkness. *Lord, wherever she is, please let her be safe.* How could she have run off? Though this wouldn't be the first time. Sounds of nearby children caught her attention. Their sweet, lighthearted voices pitched through the air with one in particular ringing familiar. They came from a neighbor's yard, but which one?

She ran across the street and rushed toward the gray-stone colonial. With her heart in her throat, hoping to find Lacy, relief flooded her, thinking sometimes she worried for nothing. Approaching the house, the gate to the back yard was unlatched. The handle lifted easily. She moved toward the voices growing louder with each step. "Lacy," she called. Laughter spilled from the opening of a large playhouse in the backyard enclosure. "Lacy?" No response. Lissa darted up to the playhouse. Inside two little girls and a playful cocker spaniel huddled over bags of candy. Her heart sank.

Lissa raced back to her car. She hopped inside, stuck her key into the ignition, and said a quick, panic-stricken prayer. It was all she could muster before pulling away in a complete frenzy. A full moon shone like a white coin through a stretch of patchy clouds. The sight couldn't have been more cliché. Halloween with its eerie glow appearing more like a manufactured stage background out of central casting.

Coasting down the street in the semi-darkness, punctuated by the golden-yellow light of the old-fashioned lampposts, Lissa's hands shook at the wheel. *Which way did I come in?* The homes at Golden Meadows sat just outside of Pinewood in a borough called Elmdale. By day, this wouldn't be an issue. Now, at dusk, the world took on an unfamiliar patina.

Her mind spun. *Lacy, where are you?* The creepy image of the white SUV suddenly came to mind again, and she shivered at the thought that she'd been followed here. He could be parked outside like the other cars and snatched Lacy when she came to wait at the curb. He could have enticed her with candy or...? Lissa didn't want to think about it. Then the maintenance guy, Mike Hemstead, flew into her head. He seemed innocuous with the cover of having a little girl. Double life? A pervert? Lissa shook off the thoughts.

Frantically, she scanned the area. Her eyes darted back and forth checking both sides of the street. The last house in the development sat on the crest of a hill above a scruffy patch of untended land adjacent to a grove of trees. Beyond the owner's property line, she glimpsed something. There. *What was that?* She slammed her foot on the brake and strained in the low light for what caught her attention. Empty beer cans and fast food wrappers littered the clearing at the edge of the development. She set the parking brake and jumped out. She ran through the weeds and debris and braced at what she saw. Three holes and black markings took the shape of an eerie grin. *Lacy's costume.*

Chapter Nineteen

Lissa's breath caught. An invisible punch hit the pit of her stomach and she couldn't breathe. On the verge of hysteria, she consciously talked to herself. *Just breathe...you need to keep breathing. In through the nose, out through the mouth.* She learned the technique in an article she read online. The practice worked well in the past whenever anxiety reached a fever pitch—whether having to speak in front of a group of people or an impromptu request to appear in her boss's office. *Stay with me, Lord.*

Lissa leaned over to wretch. Her head throbbed. With every ounce of her strength, she screamed for Lacy. Her voice keened; her heart palpitated. "Lacy," she yelled. Over and over until her vocal chords strained and felt ripped from her throat. She ran, trembling, toward the wooded area off the main roadway. Her gelatinous legs hardly keeping up with her overwhelming need to find her daughter. She raced along the perimeter, stepping over broken bottles and other trash like a wild woman. The sheet clutched to her breast. With each pathetic scream, her voice evaporated, barely making a dent in the thick night air. There was not a soul in sight. No cars. No movement. Only a surreal sense of dread.

****

"911, what is your emergency?"

Mary Cantell

"I want to report a missing child."

"Where was the child last seen?"

"At a home. In Elmdale."

"Where in Elmdale, ma'am?"

"Um, uh…I've got the address right here—okay, yes, it's 808 Larchmont. Larchmont Drive," she nervously repeated.

"Description?"

"My daughter?"

"The missing child."

"That's my daughter."

"Are you the guardian of the missing child?"

"I'm her *mother*," she said in frustration."

"Description?"

Lissa drew a blank and struggled to focus despite the chaotic whirlwind going on in her head. *Think.* "Yes, um, she's 4 ft. 3 inches, and 60 lbs. Her hair is reddish-brown—a shortish bob—and she has green eyes."

"Age?"

"She's eight."

"Birthday?"

"Her birthday is…is December 3, 1996. But—but she left there—the address I gave you. She's not there. She's gone." Lissa's voice broke. "*Please*, just send the police."

"Your location, ma'am?"

"Hold on, let me check." She twisted around to get a look at the street sign. "It's Castleview Court in the Golden Meadows Estates in Elmdale. I'm right at the entrance just off of I-70."

The light drained away from the sky and the evening air sent a chill to her arms now prickled in

110

goose flesh. A full moon shrouded in misty clouds hung like an all-knowing eye. The white sheet that was lying crumpled on the ground now eerily glowed on the front seat. The black marker smiled mockingly. *This was your idea.*

Her heart thumped wildly, and she feared she'd have a heart attack. *Just breathe...keep breathing.* The scene mirrored her eighth-grade gym class after running around the half-mile track. Toward the final lap, her lungs stretched to the max to take in oxygen, and she worried her next breath would be her last...each inhalation barely enough to satisfy her need for air. The searing ache those many years ago was no match for the emotional agony she experienced now. How much stress could a heart take?

A set of headlights traveling down Rt. 70 quickly interrupted her thoughts. *The police.* Adrenaline pulsed through her veins. *In through the nose, out through the mouth.* She ran her tongue over her raw lips, tasting blood, and envisioned rushing onto the road, signaling her location to the officer—anything to speed things up. There was no time to waste. Her anticipation rose as the headlights approached. The car barreled down the highway, not more than 300 yards away—then 200, 100, 50— The speeding car took the curve and then passed through the darkness.

Disheartened, she got back inside the car. Her mind reeled. Should she go back to the Robson home or knock on doors to see if anyone might have seen her? Head into the woods with a flashlight? Sit still and wait for the police? With every passing minute, Lissa became more desperate, like a tightrope walker without a net.

Chapter Twenty

"I'm coming right out there," Robin exclaimed.

"No, no, it's okay, Robin, I appreciate the offer, but please don't come. Brian's on his way. I just called him." Lissa didn't want or need any more confusion to dilute her attention away from the situation at hand. She could barely focus on anything as it was. More than anyone, she needed Brian. Her whole body convulsed. Her speech came out in a quiver. The sound of her best friend's voice did nothing to lessen the fear churning inside her like poisoned stew, something she needed to vomit up but couldn't. Her life spiraled into a mad descent. The hollowed out feeling inside of her could be comforted only by the sound of her daughter's voice.

"I'll be there in a heartbeat. I want to—"

"No, no, please," Lissa pleaded, hating to fend off the kind offer. "Please. I don't want you to uproot yourself on account of me. Really, I'd feel awful. I have Brian to lean on. He should be here soon."

"Okay." Robin blew a breath into the phone. "But you know I would be there for you. If you change your mind, please call me Liss."

"Yes—yes, I know."

"I understand what you're going through, honey. I've been there myself, remember?"

Lissa recalled Robin's fears when her son Alex had been caught in a well on a farm in rural Pennsylvania.

The Limerick township police department responded quickly. After four hours, they extricated the little guy from the well. Although she understood Robin sharing the worried-mother-syndrome experience, the woman's fears were no match for her own. Alex had always been in *plain* sight. Or relatively. Lissa could only imagine where Lacy was right now. All she knew was she was gone.

Robin chattered while Lissa kept her eyes and ears tuned for the police. Her friend's southern drawl soon became nothing more than blather. Lissa could no longer focus on the woman's words, and she hoped that Robin hadn't been asking her anything because she was barely able to process her words let alone respond coherently. Her jangled nerves could barely hide the quiver in her voice that mimicked the stammering of a five-year-old after a crying jag.

The lanes of I-70 curved through the trees like a long, mocking tongue. Not knowing from which direction the police or Brian would be coming, Lissa kept her gaze focused in both directions, twisting her head from side to side as though watching a tennis match. Each set of headlights gave her stomach a twinge. She wondered whether they would make the usual spectacle of using the sirens and flashing lights. The sight and sound of everyday police vehicles in full engagement mode, zooming down the road with peeling sirens and red flashing lights, was enough to make her tense until they passed. Now, on the verge of her own frenzied predicament, her tension doubled.

For a brief moment, she recalled a vivid dream where her 911 call never made it through to the police department. She could barely dial the number before something happened to the phone—either it melted, or the number wouldn't connect or misdialed. Or when she did speak to the authorities, something always kept them from arriving.

The set of headlights coming down the highway flashed with urgency. *Finally.* "Hey, Robin, the police are here."

"Okay, you better go. I'll be praying, Liss."

"Thanks."

Lissa hung up the phone wishing this was just another bad dream when the first responding officer pulled up. She didn't know whether to stay inside the car or step out to meet him. She wasn't being arrested for anything. Not wanting to be alone with a stranger, even if he was a member of the police force, her body tensed with uncertainty.

"Are you Ms. Logan?"

She nodded and stepped out of the car.

"I'm Officer Jennings." He looked down at his notebook. "Says your daughter's missing?"

"Yes, sir." Still nodding. "Please help me, Officer. She's out here—" Her panic-stricken voice bordered on hysteria as she swung her arm in a wide gesture toward the copse of trees adjacent to the development.

"Okay, you need to calm down. It's going to be okay."

"She was invited to a party, and when I went to go pick her up, they said she wasn't there. She was nowhere in the house." Her words flew out of her mouth so quickly that she realized she may have sounded like someone on cocaine. She made a conscious effort to slow down and then dissolved into tears.

"We have a description of her... eight-years-old, 4 ft. 3 inches and 60 lbs. with auburn hair and green eyes?"

"Yes, sir," she said, wailing. "She'll be nine in December. We need to find her, Officer. I'm so afraid that—"

"Not to worry, ma'am. Worrying isn't going to help us find your daughter. It'll be better for all concerned if you just kept a level head." He punctuated his words with a firm nod. "Now, I need to ask you some questions, ma'am."

The officer began asking a litany of questions just as another car pulled up behind them. Lissa recognized the car as Brian's. He threw open his door, got out, and in three strides he was by her side with his arms wrapped around her. "I'm so sorry, Liss."

"Oh, Brian," she said, latching onto him tightly.

She wiped her eyes as Brian pulled away and extended his hand to the officer. "Brian Pickering, Chief of Security, Department of Defense."

The officer nodded and with a reserved smile said, "Officer Jennings, sir. Pleased to make your acquaintance, sir." He glanced back at Lissa. "Just going over protocol here. We're almost done."

Lissa answered the remainder of the officer's questions. "Was she a happy child...? Where did she go to school...? What would make her run away?"

"She didn't run away," Lissa sobbed.

"Most all of our missing kids are runaways—"

"She wouldn't run away. She's not that kind of kid." Lissa looked up at Brian, trying to convince him, too. "Something happened to—" Lissa couldn't finish the sentence. "I—I found her costume."

"Her what?" Officer Jennings stoic face grew stern.

"Her *costume*."

"What costume?"

"From the party. Her Halloween costume. She went as a ghost." Lissa pulled open the car door and grabbed the crumpled sheet lying on the front seat. "I found it on the roadway right over there."

In the light of the overhanging street lamp, she saw a small bloodstain.

Chapter Twenty-One

"Are there any other people in your daughter's life that we should know about? An ex-husband, a caregiver, or someone you know who might want to do her harm?" Officer Jennings questioned.

Lissa, still nervously shivering, tried to focus on the officer's words. She glanced first to Brian and then back to the officer. Neither of them could help her with this. She was on her own. She shook her head. "No, no one."

"No one at all? A father, father figure, uncle—can you think of anyone?"

Lissa paused. "My husband is dead," she said, wiping her eyes. "Killed in the military." This was the first time she ever referred to her husband as *dead*. The word sounded odd and chafed her sensibilities. She wished she'd said *passed away* or *killed in action*.

The officer stared silently at her until he heard the word, *military*. He nodded and just above a whisper said, "I'm sorry to hear that, ma'am. Anyone else?"

"I have family; they live in Farmington Heights."

"Their names?"

"Charlie and Celia Rossi."

"Do you have a phone number for them?"

"Not off the top of my head, no. But I can get it for you." *Details, details. This is such a waste of time.*

"That's all right, I'll have someone check it out and

get back to you, if necessary."

Lissa's knees quivered like jelly and another chill ran through her. The lightweight denim jacket she wore along with thin cotton jeans didn't do much to keep her warm. She rubbed her hands together and tried to calm herself again through the steady breathing technique. The officer continued asking her questions, and she went on to describe the people in Lacy's life recently, including her landlady, Miss Rucker, and all the neighbors she could think of, along with some of her daughter's friends.

"Oh, wait," she began. "There was an odd thing that happened a few months ago."

The officer jotted down notes as she gave the details of the incident in July regarding the break-in along with Miss Rucker's Peeping Tom story.

"I just thought it odd is all. It's probably not even related," she said with a shrug.

"Nothing's too small to overlook, Ms. Logan." He gave her a discerning look and closed his notebook. "Chances are your daughter will be found. Many of these cases are surprisingly coincidental as to where the missing person ends up. Sometimes they're found where you least expect." He gave her an encouraging nod.

"How soon can they come out and do a search of the neighborhood?" Brian turned toward the wooded area.

"Soon as I file this report, sir, I'll get the paperwork started asap and have CED on it after that."

Lissa didn't understand and gave Brian a quizzical look.

"Criminal Enforcement Division," he explained.

Criminal. Lissa winced. The dark, dense forest adjacent to the housing development teased imposingly. The commanding trees stood like a fortress, impervious to penetration and able to swallow up a little girl without a trace. "She's in there, Brian, I know it," cried Lissa. "I'm going in there myself."

The dark pines shimmered in the breeze, lending a sharp, clean scent—the aroma she always associated with the carefree summer days spent at her grandmother's house after the floor had been mopped with pine-scented ammonia. She feared the pleasant memory would forever be usurped by this present dark and dreadful moment.

Brian pulled her back. "Liss, wait." He turned to the officer. "This could—"

"These woods—" Lissa cried out, making a sweeping gesture toward the pines, "she could be in there—anywhere."

"Officer," Brian said, "this could take hours. Could you expedite this, like now? I'll take full responsibility." As a federal employee there were certain ways to break rules that would not disrupt protocol or, hopefully, not get anyone's shorts in a knot.

****

The detective assigned to the case stood imposingly tall at the door. Dark, slicked-back hair met with the faint scent of cigarettes. The man flashed his badge and a polite professional smile. "Evening, I'm Detective Sergeant Hal Hastings, Pinewood Bureau."

Brian pulled the door back and motioned him in. He shook the tall man's hand. "I'm Brian and this is Lacy's mother, Melissa Logan." The detective nodded and then addressed her. "Sorry to hear of your little girl,

Ms. Logan."

"Thanks for coming so quickly, Detective."

"Just call me Hal. Like to keep my job a secret," he said with a wink, "if you know what I mean." He pulled out a notebook from his breast pocket and sat down on the edge of the fireplace. "So you say she was at a party, that correct?"

"Yes, sir, a Halloween party hosted by a girl named Becca Robson. A friend from Lacy's class. She's in third grade at Chilly Acres.

He made notes as Lissa spoke. "I'm assuming the kids at the party were also from the school?"

"I guess so, sir. I'm pretty sure it was Becca's birthday, so…"

"Was your daughter—"

"Lacy," interjected Lissa.

"Was Lacy in a good frame of mind when she went to the party?"

"Yes, sir, as far as I could tell."

"No angst about anything?"

She gnawed her lower lip. "No," she said, shaking her head, "not that I'm aware of. But she did mention an incident that happened to her when she was walking home the other day. Some girls—older girls, she said, blocked her from passing by."

"When was this?"

"Just last week. Just off Chilly Acres road." She raised her finger to indicate the direction. "Oh, and there was someone in a car they were talking to."

"She didn't know the girls?"

"No."

"How old were they?"

"Lacy didn't say."

"What kind of car?"

"I have no idea. Does that matter?"

"Just checking."

Lissa thought about the other day when Lacy came home out of breath, mentally retracing her conversation with her the day of the encounter. "It's yellow."

"Yellow?"

"The car. It was a yellow car."

"Yellow car," he repeated while writing.

"That's what my daughter said."

Detective Hastings continued his probe of questions as he went through his protocol checklist for missing persons. She gave him all the names of Lacy's friends and the people and places she knew Lacy frequented. He scribbled down the information and put the notebook back before standing.

"Oh, now I remember," Lissa said to him as he moved toward the door. "His name is Tommy." The detective's brow arched inquisitively. "Lacy's friend from up the street. Earlier, the policeman asked me about Lacy's friends, and I just remembered the one boy she hangs out with sometimes. I don't know his last name. And his brother is the one who was in the car."

"Hmmm…" He pulled out his notebook again and made a notation. "The yellow car, I'm assuming?"

"Yes, sir.

"Okay, well, I'll be getting the information to NCIC as well as the NCMEC data base. And if there's anything else you can think of to help the process along, just call." He handed her his business card. "Any questions, don't hesitate."

Lissa looked at him questioningly. "What's in the databases?"

"NCIC—is National Crime Information Center. NCMEC is for missing and exploited children. They're basically our lifeline," he began. "They're the national data banks for any criminal information that will lead us to your little girl, Ms. Logan." He glanced at Brian and then back to her.

"Will there—is there going to be a search party?"

"Search party, interviews…also, I'll need a picture of Lacy, preferably recent for the Amber Alert. And the sooner we get it posted in the right places, the sooner—well, the sooner the better."

"Hold on," she said, quickly slipping down the hall. She went to her bedroom closet, hoping the box of pictures stored there wasn't buried too deeply among everything else stashed inside. Surprisingly, it was on top of the others and already torn open. *When did I do that?* Inside were dozens of photos of her daughter from infancy through toddlerhood. Her fingers rifled through them in search of a more recent one. There was one of her and Lacy in a delicate gold frame atop her dresser, but she wasn't about to part with that one. Other than some candid photos of Lacy alongside other children or with the family at Christmas time, the only decent one of her alone was her second-grade class photo when she was seven.

"This is the most recent one I have," she said and handed it to the detective. Her heart dropped suddenly, realizing the reality of his request. Lacy had been kidnapped.

Chapter Twenty-Two

Unable to sit still, Lissa paced up and down the front room of her apartment. For the next hour, questions circled in her mind. How would they go about the investigation? Would the detective work alone or be assigned a team? How long was this going to take? Either way, she wanted to be involved. Panic swept through her. Every minute away from looking for her daughter was a minute wasted. She was not going to desert her.

"I want to go back, Brian," she said, anxiously, darting to the closet. "I need to be there." She slipped into her jacket, grabbed her keys, and opened the door.

"I can't just sit here and worry."

****

Several police cars formed a barrier on the road leading to the Golden Meadows estates, all with their flashers on. A K-9 unit truck sat off to the side next to a local news station's van. Pulling up to the scene felt surreal.

"The detective didn't waste any time," Brian said. "I'm impressed."

"I'm so n-nervous, Brian," Lissa, flushed with adrenaline, stammered. "I can barely talk."

"Let me do the talking then." He pulled her closer and gently warmed her hands in his.

"Thanks. I'd probably sound drunk." *I don't really*

care what they think… I just want my daughter. Lissa struggled to remind herself that this was in God's hands.

Brian pulled up to one of the officers standing by the side of the road. "Evening, Officer. I'm Brian Pickering. This is Melissa Logan, the mother of the missing child." Brian flashed his Department of Defense credentials to the police deputy on watch. "I assume the road is blocked for the investigation?"

"Yes, sir, it is."

"May we go in? We want to help in the search."

The deputy's eyebrows knit when he bent down to peer inside the car. He straightened and held up a finger. "Just a minute. Radio 331 to supervisor 123."

"Radio 123."

"Sir, I have the missing person's mother with me and—"

Brian held up his security ID, and the officer leaned forward to inspect it.

"—and a Mr. Brian Pickering."

"Pickering? DOD's Pickering?" came the static reply over the radio.

"Looks like it, sir. They say they want to assist in the search. Permission to let them through, sir?"

"Go ahead."

"Copy that." He leaned in toward the window. "Go ahead, sir."

Brian drove through the barricade and parked behind one of several police cars sprawled on the road leading to the Golden Meadows housing development. The sound of barking dogs came from somewhere in the parcel of nearby woods. Another stab of panic hit her gut. They got out of the car, and she latched onto

Brian's arm as they made their way over to one of the officers on duty.

"Evening, sir," Brian said. "I'm Brian Pickering, and this is Melissa Logan, the missing girl's mother."

"Evening, I'm Sgt. Matthews."

"We were looking for Detective Hastings," Brian said.

"Hastings? He's around here somewhere. I'll page him."

A sickening chill ran through her despite the warmth of Brian's body next to hers. *Lacy, where are you? Why did you run away?*

The night sky held a scattering of stars that glowed bright as neon. Above the horizon, she spotted the seven stars of the Big Dipper. A moment of déjà vu hit. Constellations were always a puzzle to her with the plethora of stars sprinkled across the great wide expanse of night sky. She wondered if Lacy was somewhere in the woods or on her way home and looking at the night sky, too. Did she see the Big Dipper? Was she being guided by the North Star back home or was she lost? Either way, Lissa knew amid the darkness, the creator of the moon and stars had his eye on her daughter. It was the only comfort she derived at this moment. *God, please lead her.*

"He's over on the other side," Sgt. Matthews said, pointing. "Told him you were looking for him."

Brian nodded. "How wide is the search?"

The officer held a flashlight over a map of the county. "We're right here by the red *X*. These woods run for the next 1800 yards or so right up to Piney Creek. We'll take it as far as the creek where it meets up with I-85."

"How many on the rescue squad?"

"I've got all my expendable men on duty right now. We have SAR dogs and the state police from Howard, and we've called Carroll's jurisdictions... should be here soon. We're on top of it."

"What about the people in the housing development, will they be interviewed?"

"Hastings should be on that. You can ask him—there is he is now."

With his lanky stride, Detective Hastings stepped out of the shadows. His slow measured pace reminded her of a stork making its way out of marshy water. *Doesn't he know every second counts?*

"Detective," Brian called out, before she had the chance, from where they stood under the lamp post and signaled with his hand.

"We meet again," the detective said as he approached.

"Yeah, um, she—*we* couldn't just sit around—"

"We're here to help. If that's all right," Lissa interjected.

"Can't stop you." He took a final drag on his cigarette and tossed it to the ground. "Actually, I need all the help I can get." He blew out a trail of smoke and glanced in the direction of Sgt. Matthews. "No offense, Matthews."

"None taken, Hastings."

The detective turned to Lacy and Brian. "We have a long history," he said just above a whisper. "But we have each other's backs just the same."

"Find anything?" Matthews asked.

Detective Hastings shook his head and mashed the tossed butt with his shoe. "So far, we've come up dry."

"Nothing?" he inquired, grim-faced.
"Not yet."

Chapter Twenty-Three

"Polygraph?" Lissa exclaimed. "Why on earth do I need to take a polygraph test?"

"I'm sorry, Ms. Logan," the detective said, dryly. "It's standard protocol."

Lissa stared at him in disbelief, her blood pressure rising. "I can't believe this. You think that I—somehow, I'm responsible for this? Is that what you're saying?" Incredulous, she pointed to her chest. *This is ludicrous.*

"Most of these cases turn out to be domestic in nature," said the detective.

"Well, not this one."

Brian put his arm around her. "Liss, it's not a big deal. You take the test, and it's all done. You prove your innocence. Painless."

Lissa inwardly balked at the insult. "But I have nothing to prove here. I'm her mother for Pete's sake—not like some crazy…" She stopped herself. She didn't want to implicate anyone.

Detective Hastings lit another cigarette. "Doesn't have to be right now, we can schedule it tomorrow or the next day. Not a problem."

Tomorrow or the next day? I don't think I can live past tonight if we don't find you, Lacy. Please God, ordain my steps.

Her gaze followed his hand as he took a drag and

blew the smoke out. She squelched the urge to snatch it from him and yell he should be doing more to find Lacy. She found it hard to breathe.

"You up to speaking to the press?" he asked, breaking into her thoughts.

****

Channel 11 news…live, local, late breaking. The graphics burst onto the TV along with the theme music. Lissa's breath caught at the sound of the trumpet crescendo and the fast pan of the camera to everyday slice-of-life scenes all over the county—a kid eating water ice, a horse being fed in a stable, a girl scout troop lined up to board a bus—and, of course, a dog. Next to babies, dogs owned a monopoly on cuteness over and above anything. She turned up the volume.

"I don't know whether this is the top story or not," she said. "We might have to sit through most of this broadcast before it airs."

When Detective Hastings suggested she go home and he'd contact her if anything new came in, she couldn't leave. She had a desperate urgency to stay planted right there—the place where Lacy had last been. Just in case by some slight chance her daughter was found inside the woods—dead or alive—Lissa wanted to be there for Lacy. Through the urging of both Brian and the detective, she grudgingly left.

The dark-haired male and blonde female anchor duo alternately read the copy and jovially bantered during the newscast. Then a solemn expression overcame the blonde as she began the story of the missing child. *Here it comes.* Lissa's stomach dropped when a picture of Lacy appeared on the screen. The news people cropped the color photo and enlarged it to reveal just her head. When picture day rolled around at school, Lissa recalled Lacy wanting to wear her new pink Little Princess T-shirt, but she ended up changing her top at Lissa's encouragement. A stab of guilt hit her at the thought of Lacy never wearing her favorite T-shirt again. The picture disappeared from the screen and segued into the interview with the reporter.

"Mrs. Logan, do you have any idea where your daughter could be right now?" the fresh-faced reporter dressed to the nines in professionally applied makeup asked.

"No—no idea at all," she replied softly.

I look horrible. "I wish he never talked me into that interview." Lissa lamented, cringing at her ghastly pale image under the bright camera lights.

Her gaze glued to the TV as if reliving an out-of-body experience. She hoped the viewing audience saw her demeanor as genuine, garnering a sympathetic reaction, not one of judgment that she may have been just one more half-crazed loony responsible for the disappearance.

The reporter asked her several more questions. Lissa nodded and attempted to keep calm, but the tremor in her voice indicated her desperation.

"I—I just want to say," she began, steeling herself under the harsh camera lights, "I want to say, please. Please give me my Lacindra—my Lacy," she said, correcting herself into the microphone. "Please… just…wherever she is, whoever you are that has her, please bring her back to me… I need…I want my little—" Her voice broke with the strain of emotion pressing in from all sides.

As strong as she tried to be in front of the camera,

her eyes filled with tears. She struggled to keep her face from awkwardly crumbling but lost the fight.

"Oh, cut away already," she yelled at the screen that captured her breaking down at the podium.

"You look fine, Liss, considering everything." Brian put his arm around her. Normally, his touch would have melted her into a puddle. Now, anxiety simmering, her senses dulled to his touch. The scene cut back to the anchor desk. She clicked off the TV. She couldn't sit through any more, much less watch the pretense of the news readers feign a concern they didn't really own. Her daughter could be dead for all they truly cared, despite their worried expressions.

"Brian, I don't think I can stand another minute of sitting here. I'll never be able to sleep." She folded and unfolded her arms across her chest, not finding a suitable position for them. Her body charged with energy that begged to be released.

"Liss, there's not much we can do ourselves. Just let the cops do their work. You've got to trust that they're doing what they can," he told her.

"I feel so helpless." She shook her hands nervously. "I need to do something."

"But you've got help. There's a competent detective working as we speak. And, you've got the Pinewood police force along with the help of the other counties, Howard, and Carroll, too. The detective himself gave you his word he'd call with breaking news, right?"

Lissa pictured all the people dispatched to where Lacy disappeared and hoped they'd find her soon. At least, a clue. She wondered why Lacy had discarded her ghost costume. Did she leave it behind as a clue? Was she alone in all of this? Was she being chased? Lissa's mind raced with one horrible scenario after another.

With the celebrity of the situation, the whole county now knew. Her face had been splashed over the news channels, and bulletins were being announced by radio. Had they seen her? Would they rise out of the comfort of their homes to help look for her? Would they care?

A tumult of emotion and rage rose inside her. Something evil happened at the Robson home. Like a prop in a movie set, all was not what it seemed inside the well-appointed house. She berated herself for her decision to let Lacy go to the party. The bad mommy demon plagued her while her thoughts telescoped back to the past several hours. Lissa imagined an alternative evening—an invitation to Uncle Charlie and Aunt Celia's house. Surely, she'd have been safe with them. They would have gone trick-or-treating and then returned home. This nightmare would never have happened. The demon circled around her, taunting her with a picture of what could have been if she had been more insistent.

Lissa ran to Lacy's room and flung herself on top of her bed. The weight of her anguish pressed like a vice. She wanted to die.

****

Detective Hastings snuffed out his cigarette at the curb. "No sign? Nothing? Is that what you're saying?"

"No scent...the dogs couldn't pick up a thing... that's what the K-9 unit said," Officer Jennings explained. "Maybe Sergeant Matthews has a more recent update but that's what I heard, sir."

Detective Hastings thought about his next move,

which would be to start knocking on doors in the immediate neighborhood. He got in his car and began with the first house adjacent to the parcel of woods.

"Evening." He flashed his badge. "Have a word with you?"

The short man wearing boxers and a T-shirt pulled the door open.

"Hope it's not too late. Saw your light on." He shrugged. "Thought I'd take a chance."

"Anything the matter, Officer?"

"Detective. Detective Hastings."

"Detective. Yes, sir," the man repeated, nervously.

"Not a problem. Sorry to bother you so late but…" He let his words dissolve and pulled out his notebook and pen. "Just have a few questions for you. Won't take long."

"Have we done something wrong?"

"Depends," the detective replied. "Have you seen a little girl this evening? Eight years old, reddish-brown hair?"

He curled his lips downward. "I—I don't know. All the kids who came to our door had costumes on." He turned to the woman standing next to him. "Honey, do we know her?"

Puzzled, the woman replied. "Every kid's head was covered. At least as far as I know."

"You sure?"

She nodded with certainty. "I'm sure."

Just then the detective's phone rang. "Excuse me," he said to the couple, holding his hand over the phone. "Okay. Got it. Great." He hung up and turned back to them. "If you do see her, here's my card. Have a good evening."

****

"Liss?" Brian called from the doorway. The only light in the dark room came from the tiny glow of a pink nightlight on the wall in the shape of a tiny poodle. He stepped toward the bed where she lay face down, curled in a fetal position. "Liss, listen to me," he said, gently rubbing his hand along her back.

As much as she loved him, even the sound of his voice could not persuade her to move. She wanted to be alone, to burrow inward and shut everything out, including Brian. The world and everything in it meant nothing at that moment. She wanted to spiral to where the pain couldn't find her and longed for God to take her—right then and there.

"If I can't have my daughter, there's nothing to live for," she said, choking out the words muffled by her emotions.

"Your cell rang while you were in here," he said. "I answered. It was Hal."

Hal? She remembered the detective mentioning his first name, but for her, he'd always be *Detective.*

"He said there's a lady…and she has information."

A ray of hope sparked inside her; she opened her eyes and turned over. "A lady? Who? What kind of information?" She propped hrself up on one elbow.

"He didn't say. Only they got a call from someone. A woman in Elmdale."

"She knows something?"

"Hal said to meet him there."

"Where?" she demanded.

"The lady's house."

As though a switch turned on, a surge of energy released in her. "He wants us to go to her house now?

Where does she live?"

"I wrote it down." He handed her the paper.

"I can't see…turn on the light," she said, and Brian sat up and reached for the switch on the wall.

"722 Larchmont in Elmdale? That's the Robsons' street," she said with excitement and bolted off the bed.

Chapter Twenty-Four

On the ride from Pinewood to Elmdale, Lissa kept her eyes peeled to the sides of the roadway, desperately darting her sight in both directions looking for Lacy along the way. At the approach to the Golden Meadows estates, her heart rate quickened as Brian made the turn off I-70 into the development at Castleview Court.

"Larchmont is around here somewhere," she said. "Keep going…there—on the right."

Brian drove through the stately homes in the development and Lissa squinted to make out the addresses. "There's 808," she said, pointing to the mailbox. "The Robsons." Aside from the tiny orange-glow lanterns along the fieldstone walkway, their imposing house stood completely dark. *Lacy is missing, and you have the nerve to go to bed?* "Sleep tight, Jay and Janet," she said under her breath.

Brian turned to her. "You say something?"

"Nothing, just talking to myself."

They drove to the end of the block where the development ended at the intersection with Rt. 13 near Old Orchard Lake.

"Oh, for Pete's sake, where is 722?"

"It must be somewhere in the next block," he said.

When they crossed the road, Larchmont Drive turned into Larchmont Lane where older, more modest looking homes dwelled among thick stands of trees. In the darkness lit only by the moon, an eclectic blend of A-frames and small ranch-style homes nestled in large plots on top of land that retained its original natural charm and character. The preserved land hadn't been cleared to make way for a developer's dream of creating a burb for the nouveau riche. At least, not yet.

"It's so dark, I can't make out the numbers," she said in frustration. "Can you see them?"

"Not really, but it looks like that might be the detective's car up ahead on the left."

Moments later, the door to a black SUV opened and a tall skinny figure stepped out. The sight of the detective's vehicle resembled a movie prop. *Didn't they all drive black SUVs?*

A running tape threaded through her mind again; the scenario of what could have played out if Lacy had gone to Aunt Celia and Uncle Charlie's for Halloween instead of Becca's party. She paused to recall what day it was. Sunday? Monday? Her mind swirled. What if she'd picked her up sooner instead of dawdling on the phone with Robin? Though, deep down she knew this wasn't her fault. Lacy was a carefree spirit, sometimes losing track of time and worrying Lissa to the point of distraction, but this was not one of her pleasant diversions or episodes of side-tracked lateness. With each passing moment, she pictured the worst thing imaginable. She struggled with her own imagination and fought, once again, to shed the horrible images from her head.

Brian leaned in closer. "We'll find her, Liss." He squeezed her hand and gently wrapped his arms around her. "Just breathe."

The scent of cigarette smoke drifted through the

night air as the detective approached their car in his stork-legged stride.

"Hey, Hal," Brian said as he rolled down the window.

"Evening. Okay, lady's name is Lydia Petruzzi," he told them, pulling out his notebook. "Her call came right after the ten o'clock news. Sounded pretty normal—not like some of these nut jobs who give you the run around and sound like they got a screw loose, ya know what I'm sayin'? But I could be wrong. Can't tell you how many wrong numbers I've had to deal with over the years." He shook his head. "People are kooky, I tell ya. Already been up this side of the street for the past hour." He indicated the direction somewhere on the newer end of Larchmont. "Was about to head over here when my phone rang. The station said there were about a half-dozen calls with sightings so far."

"A half-dozen," Lissa exclaimed, her hope coming alive again. "Already?"

Hal nodded. "We'll check 'em out, but…" He snapped his notebook shut. "I'm not expecting much. Gonna check the local hospital soon—just in case. It takes a while before the real ones come along. A lot of the early ones turn out to be bogus."

Her hope deflated.

The detective and Brian took the lead as they walked along the dark street to the front door of Lydia Petruzzi's tiny rancher set among a cluster of too tall pines. One lightning storm and the fall of even one of the trees could smash the poor woman's roof in. Lissa saw the curtain move at the side window followed by the door opening. A short, rotund woman in her mid-to-late 60s with jet black hair threaded with gray and kind eyes peered out from behind it.

"Ms. Petruzzi? I'm Detective Hal Hastings, and this is Ms. Logan and Mr. Pickering."

"The mother of the little girl?" She beckoned them inside. "I'm so glad you came." She clasped her hands together, saying, "I have coffee," as though preparing to perform an opera solo.

Detective Hastings politely shook his head and waved away the suggestion.

"Or tea, would you prefer some tea? I have some biscotti—"

"No, no," he interrupted politely, "but thank you, Ms. Petruzzi. Very kind of you but we won't be staying long."

This isn't a social call, Lissa thought. The woman's kindness reminded her of her mother's side of the family—particularly Aunt Celia, who always demonstrated the need to feed everyone. *Salt of the earth.*

"We're here to find out," he began, exchanging glances with Lissa, "about Ms. Logan's daughter."

"Oh, yes, such a pity that she's missing," she said, leading them into the kitchen. "Please sit down." She pointed toward the table. "Please, sit down—all of you."

The kitchen walls, painted in pale blue, held copper molds, and trails of ivy grew in containers on a low dividing partition between the kitchen and dining room. Lissa hadn't seen such old-fashioned décor since last visiting her grandmother decades ago before she passed away. A statue of the Virgin Mary stood in the corner; in the shadowy lighting, the figure appeared eerily life-like.

"Now, Ms. Petruzzi, I just wanted to confirm that you called the Amber Alert number," Detective Hastings said, his pen poised above his notebook. "You said you had some information, a tip for where to find the missing child, Lacy Logan?"

"Ms. Logan," she began, turning to Lissa, who remained in the doorway despite the woman's invitation to sit. "I think I saw your daughter." She paused. "But I can't be sure. I just thought it prudent to alert the police because it might have been her and then again maybe not. Our eyes do tricks on us. I know that for a fact."

Detective Hastings tapped his pen on his thigh. "Where did you see her, Ms. Petruzzi?"

"Earlier this evening, I was on Rt. 70 at Shady Grove, not far from the lake."

"Do you remember the time?"

"I don't recall exactly but I was coming home from Fielding's market—I didn't have any candy for the children, so I went out to buy some. By the time I got back, I'd say it was getting close to six-thirty."

"Where did you see her? Was she walking by herself?"

"When I stopped for a red light, I noticed a little girl about yea high," she said, indicating with her hand. "She was walking alongside the fence by the road. Then the little girl turned her head. It appeared someone may have called to her because she quickly ran over to their car."

"What was she wearing?" the detective asked.

"Did she have a ghost costume on?" Lissa interjected. "Or was she carrying a sheet?"

Ms. Petruzzi looked doubtful and shook her head.

"No, no sheet. She had…um, I think it was a striped shirt—blue and white—yes, a blue and white striped shirt. That's about all I recall, really."

Lissa's stomach lurched. Lacy had clothes matching the woman's description, though so did a lot of people. Striped shirts were ubiquitous. She tried to recall what Lacy was wearing underneath her costume. When she stepped out of her bedroom just before leaving for the party, her ghost costume was already on. The only thing Lissa noticed was her daughter's faded blue jeans and scuffed barely white Keds sneakers. Or maybe some other pants? At this point, her mind turned back into mush.

"So, Ms. Petruzzi, what happened at the car? Did someone talk with her? Did you notice any impression on the child's face?"

The woman opened and then closed her mouth, struggling how to respond.

"Okay," the detective said and shifted in his chair. "Let's begin with the car. What happened at the stoplight after you saw the child go over to the car?"

Mrs. Petruzzi's eyes enlarged. "I saw her get into it."

"She got in. Okay. Did you notice whether she looked, possibly, forced into the car, or did she go in voluntarily?"

"Um, it looked like she knew the person inside the car because it wasn't long before she went inside."

"What kind of car was it? Do you remember the make or model?"

She shook her head. "No, I don't know either, really. I'm so sorry, detective." She glanced over to Brian and then let her gaze settle on Lissa. "I'm sorry,

141

but I don't know makes and models of cars. I've never been good at that sort of thing. My late husband loved model cars—he had a hobby of building them—poor soul is gone to Heaven now but he—"

"So you don't know whether it was a new or late model?" the detective interrupted.

"No, sir, I'm sorry." She folded her hands as though about to say grace for dinner.

The detective twisted in the chair.

"But I can tell you what color it was," she said, brightening.

Lissa, who'd been hanging on the woman's every word, strained to hear.

"What color?" the detective asked.

"It was a very odd color," she began. "It was yellow. Bright yellow, like a jar of mustard."

A burning sensation sputtered up in Lissa's throat. She turned and ran out of the kitchen and then out the front door into the night.

****

Lissa heard Brian's voice in the distance calling her as he came up the sidewalk. She wanted to respond to him but didn't have the strength even though the nauseous feeling had passed. His footsteps came quickly as he jogged toward the car and got in.

"Liss, honey," he said, breathless, when he got there. "Why'd you run out?"

"I'm a mess, Brian. I'm sorry...but when she—she said a *yellow* car, it just struck me hard. I think I know who did this. Or might have...I don't know." She held a hand to her forehead.

"You think it's the same yellow car you said Lacy mentioned?"

She shrugged. "How many yellow cars are in this town?"

"It might be significant. I'm sure it's not lost on the detective. But in the meantime, I better take you home."

Lissa shook her head. "No, I'm all right now. I just needed some air. It felt like the walls of that lady's kitchen were about to close in on me. And all of those gargoyle things…" She shuddered. "Eww."

"You look pale, Liss. You're going to run yourself down, and then what good will you be? To anyone. Let me take you home. Tomorrow, we can—"

"I can't rest now, Brian, I'm too wired. What about the detective? Is he coming?"

"I don't know how much longer he'll be." Brian rolled down the window. "Wait, here he comes now."

Lissa wished he would walk faster as he ambled up the sidewalk. *And ditch the cigarettes, too. I don't need you to die on me from lung cancer.*

"You okay, Ms. Logan?" the detective asked, bending down to the level of the window.

"Detective—" her voice now rising with excitement, "—the yellow car…I know who owns it. Remember, I told you about it before? Lacy mentioned the color of the car parked on the street the day she was—was, I don't know—stonewalled, I guess, by that girl on her way home from school. She said there was—"

"A yellow car," he said, finishing her sentence.

"Yes, we need to check that out, sir."

Chapter Twenty-Five

At 6:47 p.m., police officer Dwayne McCall pulled up to the accident scene; the sight of crumpled metal sent a punch to his stomach. What was left of the torn-up vehicle had been moved off to the side leaving shards of broken glass and debris in the roadway. With only one lane reopened, traffic crawled through the area. The delay was compounded by everyone gawking at the horrific mess. Even more unnerving, the officer noticed something intriguing within the wreckage. One of the cars looked familiar. A medical helicopter sat on the roadway, the rotary wings spinning. He watched them carry a stretcher and load it into the aircraft before stepping out of his squad car.

****

"The patient is secure." The paramedic wiped his brow and turned to the pilot. "Any cautions?"

Pilot Jason Hardy focused on the control panel. "No cautions. All clear. All instruments in the green."

"I've started the Sentanyl," called the nurse, while checking the IV.

"Fuel?"

"One hour-fifty minutes."

"Engines?"

"Two to fly."

"Okay."

"We're in flight mode. EMS-38 1 is lifting with

four souls on board. Inbound for Holy Cross."

"Patient looks to be in his mid-to-upper thirties," the nurse said. "I hope he makes it."

****

"Hey, some crash," Officer McCall called to one of the other patrolman on duty after pulling up to the scene. "Nasty."

"You could say that," the patrolman replied. "We got 340 still closed—all lanes. I just happened to be on I-70 when it happened—traveling west myself. Saw it happen. Scared the heck out of me. If it weren't for the no U-turn sign, one of the cars could've clipped me good."

Officer McCall turned around to look at the highway. "What U-turn sign?"

"My point exactly. It flew—somewhere. The car just missed me by a hair."

"Heard there was a pile up. How many?"

"Yep. There was an eighteen-wheeler," he said, pointing about fifty yards down the roadway where the mammoth truck jackknifed. "It must have slipped on some oil or something, who knows? And then another couple of cars slid into him. And on the other side of the highway, coming out of cross traffic, a taxi cab slammed into the whole pile of 'em."

"Collision between an eighteen-wheeler, two cars, and a taxi? Good night. Anything suspicious about it?"

"I don't know, sir. I expect it'll all come out in the investigation."

"How many got airlifted?"

"Just one, sir. And an ambulance took another one. Unfortunately, there were two fatalities."

The officer stared toward the pile of wreckage on

the side of the road, wondering how anyone even survived.

****

"Emergency trauma three," the lead nurse called out when the EMS team bolted through the door of Holy Cross hospital.

"Right ac joint and a 14-gauge on his right hand," the paramedic announced. "With 80 systolic. He lost a lot of blood in the accident."

"Anything for the pain?" the lead nurse asked.

"Base suggested morphine. Five mgs administered so far."

"Got it," she said, taking notes. "Any family here?"

"Not that I know of." He shook his head. "Bad accident."

The patient was transferred to one of the bays and like a choreographed dance, the ER trauma team jumped into action. An assistant set up a chest tube monitor while another assistant drew blood.

"Breath is decreased," the surgeon said. "He may need a CT scan when his vitals are stable. Keep me posted on any changes."

"Doesn't appear to be any brain hemorrhage but…"

"Vitals are steady."

"Airway is open."

"Get a scan."

Chapter Twenty-Six

Celia turned on the bedroom TV and waited for the mud mask on her face—*guaranteed to soften lines and wrinkles*—to dry and harden. "Charlie, is that you?" Celia called when she heard the familiar sound of the front door closing. She quickly rinsed off the mask and patted her face dry. Downstairs, her husband sat at the kitchen table chomping a sugar cookie. A glass of milk and a section of newspaper lay on the table in front of him.

"I thought they served dinner at the Legion Hall?

"They did," he said through a mouthful. "But I didn't eat much—wasn't hungry for some reason. Until now."

"It's not good to eat so late. Not just before bedtime. And why *were* you so late? It's after ten. I was getting worried."

"There was some kind of commotion on the road. A bunch of road flares were set up on 340 and a cop was redirecting traffic. He made us turn around, so I had to take the long way home or come home by way of West Virginia. I took the shortcut through Petersen's farm."

"That must have been the accident they were talking about on the news," she said. "Glad you weren't in it." She placed a peck on his cheek and took the empty glass to the sink. After rinsing and setting it in the dishwasher, she wiped the sink with a paper towel and put in the drain stopper before heading back upstairs.

****

"A yellow car? Ms. Logan, I don't know how we'll be able to—" the detective began.

"Can you please just check it out? I know exactly where it is, the house is right up on—oh, I forget the name of the street, but I know where to find it."

"Ms. Logan, it's mighty late." Detective Hastings stubbed his cigarette on the curb and clicked open the door to his SUV.

"I know it's late, sir, but—"

"Liss," Brian interjected. "Better to wait until morning to buttonhole people rather than wake them up. It's almost midnight."

"Ms. Logan, he's right. Even I—"

"But I know someone in that house may have taken my daughter. I can't wait much longer. This is our only clue," she cried, her energy sparking to life.

"Even if you know who might be responsible for this, it's not the best time to interrogate him—or her," the detective said.

"He's right, Liss. Better wait for a reasonable hour."

She glared at both of them. "If you don't go, I will."

"Tell you what, Ms. Logan." Detective Hastings raised his hand in surrender. "I'll make a deal with you. Go home, get some sleep, and I'll pick you up tomorrow morning seven a.m. sharp. Deal?"

Lissa could see she was up against a wall. It wasn't like these men weren't on her side but she needed to be taken seriously. She cupped her face in her palms. She prayed for God's will to be done and to give her the wisdom to do the right thing. During her prayer, a warm feeling spread through her limbs and the queasiness in her stomach eased. With all the pleas she'd uttered before, this was the first time she'd been physically moved by one.

"Ms. Logan?"

She looked up.

"Okay, Ms. Logan?"

Lissa released a sigh and nodded begrudgingly. "Okay, seven a.m. sharp. I'll be outside waiting."

The detective gave her a decided look, tugged his tie, and took a step backward toward his car. He pointed a finger at her. "You got it."

Chapter Twenty-Seven

Lissa stared at the alarm clock. The room, so silent she could hear the whisper of the digits as they flipped… 2:01, 2:02. With each passing moment, her desperation grew. Time was truly her enemy, and the night became all the more menacing for what remained hidden. *Where are you?* The only solace she could find was that God knew. The minutes ticked by and scraped her nerves raw. She cried out, "God, please bring her home."

She coiled in a fetal position; her body tensed. Along with the image of her daughter's face, the driver of the yellow car loomed in her mind. *Did he play a part in this?* Caught in the dissonance between wanting to find Lacy herself and having to wait for professional help, the frustration only intensified her resolve. Her desperation stole any ability to sleep. The down filled comforter on top of her bed lent little comfort now even after taking a melatonin tablet chased by chamomile tea. Despite her need for sleep, there would be no rest tonight. She felt locked in a box with no windows or door. No way out. *Is this some kind of penance, Lord?*

Lissa checked her phone. Two calls came in just before midnight. One from her Aunt Celia and one from an unknown number in Elmdale. It would be too late to call back now. Another glimpse of the clock revealed that time appeared to slow down. She lay curled on the bed, phone in hand. and stared at the time as her nerves, on edge, prickled underneath her skin.

Wired, she got up and paced. The worn floorboards flexed and squeaked under her feet as she moved restlessly around the apartment. Like an automaton, she roamed from room to room, drawn to the windows where she held out a glimmer of hope of finding something outside in the darkness to relieve the potent ache in her chest. She scanned the street, straining for the figure of a child's moving shadow or the flashing lights of a police car to distract her from the bitter anxiety now soaking into her bones. The night remained quiet. Everything and everyone safely tucked in. Nothing short of having Lacy home and safely under her pink satin bed cover would make a dent in repairing her crumbling heart.

Lissa went to Lacy's room. In the glow of the nightlight, the sight of her daughter's empty bed brought another pang of guilt. She ran her hand across the soft, cool satin and then moved to Lacy's desk, presently cluttered with a stack of library books, assorted crayons and markers, and back issues of American Girl magazine. She turned on the desk lamp and opened the top drawer. Among several colored pencils and erasers sat her white leather-bound one-year diary Lissa had purchased for her when they shopped for school supplies back in September. The scent of its leather, still fresh. Lissa valued her daughter's privacy, but there was something about the tiny leather journal that tempted her to open it. The diary came with a little key to keep the contents private but apparently Lacy hadn't locked it. The key remained taped to the front cover in the original sealed plastic. She opened the diary and began reading…

Monday, October 3 ~ Had fun in school today. Met a new girl named Julia and we walked home together.

Tuesday, October 4 ~ Miss Keogan praised me in class for my report on Daddy and Grandpop. Good day.

Thursday, October 13 ~ Julia was sick today. Walked home alone. A girl was mean to me on the way home. She said my family caused trouble in this town. Saw Tommy's brother there sitting in his ugly yellow car.

Lissa stared at the words her daughter wrote. Her heart began to palpitate. *Trouble? What on earth…?*

Just after the sun rose came a knock at the door. Finally, the dreaded night had passed. Lissa didn't think the avalanche of grief and regret that poured out from her soul through her anguished cries would ever slow. All night long, the imposed respite from the search kept her handicapped—confined in her own cell block of emotional turmoil. Whoever was behind the door was either Brian or the detective, and she welcomed the relief of another human being, someone who could erase the enigma of her daughter's disappearance. The energy within her to conquer this nightmare she was locked into began to simmer once more.

Ten minutes to seven, ahead of the detective, Brian stood at the door in a fresh button-down shirt and khakis. When Lissa answered, she fell into his arms.

"Long night, I know," he said, pulling her close.

Still dressed in the same jeans from the night before, she trembled in his arms. As much as she cared deeply for Brian, she would have traded him or anyone at that moment for a hug from her child. She longed to inhale the scent of crayons and grape bubblegum that sometimes lingered in her hair. Lacy's birthday was in less than a month. She would be nine in December. The horror of the situation smacked her once more.

Like a bad dream, the last seven hours were surreal. The separation from her only child numbed her senses and she hovered somewhere outside the moment. To accept the reality would be too much to bear. She knew God was guiding her, holding her heart. There was no way she would be able to handle this situation and still remain sane without the Lord's presence with her. Although Brian held her in his arms, she sensed it was the Lord holding both of them.

"Were you able to get any sleep?" he asked, a sweet tenderness in his voice.

"Ask the bags under my eyes." Strips of purple below her eyes told the story by way of the fluorescent-lit bathroom mirror. She caught a peek of her reflection sometime after three a.m. and gasped at the sight.

She pulled from his embrace. "These," she said, picking up her tortoise-framed sunglasses from the table, "will cover a multitude of sins."

A half-eaten piece of toast sat on the counter next to a half-filled glass of orange juice. Next to the plate lay the diary.

"I'm glad you at least had something to eat," he said.

"I tried, but I have no appetite."

"I stopped for coffee and a couple of cream cheese bagels. The bags are in the car if you want some for later." He shoved his hands into his pockets.

"That was sweet of you, thanks." Is the detective here?"

"It's not quite seven, yet," he said, glancing at his

watch.

Lissa put on her jacket and went to the window. She lifted one of the slats in the dusty blinds and knew she needed to clean them. As much as she coveted cleanliness, right now, she couldn't have cared less. "I hope he's coming soon. I'll walk to that stupid house if I have to."

"Liss," Brian consoled. "He said he'd be here. He wants to find Lacy just as much as you do."

"Just as much? I don't think so." She picked up her cell phone and keys.

"That yours?" he asked, pointing to the diary the counter.

"No. Lacy's. There's something in there I want to show the detective." She tucked it under her arm. "I'm ready. Let's go."

Chapter Twenty-Eight

The sun struggled to break free from a scrim of opal-colored clouds the first morning of November. Cars drove up and down Bellevue Avenue the same as any ordinary day. People stood waiting for the bus or walked their pets—all content in their own little worlds; no one the wiser as to the upheaval in hers.

Lissa could barely contain the heady rush of emotions going on inside her body. The excitement, trepidation, and heartache together churned in a cauldron of anxiety. She looked at Brian, so grateful for his support; both yesterday evening and now today he'd taken the day off to assist in the search. His very presence, a gift. She understood the commitment of a spouse or fiancé in matters like this, but his loyalty went above and beyond anything she would have expected of him. Was it out of his feelings for her or merely the pressing call of duty, the possibility of becoming a hero? Did he have an allegiance to the cause, or was it something else?

Just then, Mrs. Houser's son, Drew, came around the side of the house with little Toby in tow. Apparently, he had the job of taking Miss Rucker's Shih Tzu out for a walk in the morning before school. It was Lacy's responsibility in the afternoon. *Did she even know about Lacy's disappearance?* With a headset on, the boy appeared oblivious to his surroundings. Lissa didn't even bother to wave. She gave up attempting to be polite to anyone wearing a listening device after so many times of being snubbed with them not even aware of her presence.

Now, a block away, Lissa spotted the detective's black SUV slowly making its way up the street. *Like a hearse*. The SUV pulled up and stopped.

"Morning," the detective said, coming around to meet them at the curb.

"Any more leads come in, sir?" Brian inquired.

"I've got a bunch I'm still going through. Just spoke to my duty officer who's keeping tabs on them. I'll check in with him later after this." He addressed Lissa. "Okay, what's the game plan, Ms. Logan?" He pulled the cigarette from his mouth and a cloud of smoke filled the air around him. "You coming along?"

"I've been ready since yesterday," she said, zipping up her jacket.

"This is a bit unorthodox for me. I usually work solo...but whatever." He took another drag. "Okay, last night you mentioned a yellow car. So where do we find it? Got the address?"

"I'm not sure of the exact street number but I can tell you how to get there. It's not far."

He dropped the cigarette to the ground. "Good enough," he said, mashing it with his shoe. "Hop in."

Once inside the warm interior, Lissa didn't waste any time and quickly paged through Lacy's diary. "The entry on October 13th," she said, handing the diary to him. She pointed to the first line. "Does that bother you at all?"

Detective Hastings took the diary and squinted for a moment. "Okay, let's see now...you mean the word *trouble* here?"

"Yes." She nodded. "It sounds odd to me. First of all…that a girl would be in my daughter's face for no apparent reason."

"How do you know there wasn't a reason?" the detective questioned. "There doesn't always have to be a reason."

"I know my daughter," she said, raising her voice emphatically. "Besides, I asked her if she had any idea why the girl would have approached her like that and she had no clue whatsoever. Then I read *this* in her diary. The girl has some kind of vendetta or something, I don't know."

"Sounds like kids being kids to me. Takes all kinds, you know." He looked at the diary and then back at her. "You never had a bully bother you?"

Her seventh grade homeroom classmate, Carmen Costillo, a girl with oily brown hair and shabby clothes who lived in the slums of Bryn Mawr, came close. She had the word *nasty* written all over her and was often seen hanging out in the girls' bathroom between classes throughout junior high, always smelling of cigarette smoke. After school one day, she cornered Lissa outside. Frightened by the girl's smirking attitude, she ran back inside straight into the arms of her homeroom teacher who went outside and told the girl to move along.

"Yeah, I guess so," she replied.

"I'd like to keep this for evidence—just in case." He held up the diary. "Okay with you?"

She nodded.

Detective Hastings disengaged the break and pulled into the street. Lissa directed him up Bellevue

Avenue. The neighborhood's grand Victorians stood proudly on their emerald parcels of lawn.

"I think we should make a right turn here," she said. They drove for two more blocks and at the next corner, she pointed. "There it is," she announced. "The one with the turret."

The detective pulled up to the home and turned off the engine. The name on the dingy pewter mailbox read: *Hellinger*.

****

"Jay," cried Jan Robson. "The little girl, Lacy Logan. The police are involved. They're conducting a search."

With razor in hand and half-shaven, Jay Robson rushed into the bedroom where his wife sat on the bed staring at the TV. "The newscast just now…they're looking for her. I feel so awful about it, I want to die." Her face folded. "It's our fault, Jay. It's entirely our fault."

Jay stood silent for a moment, recalling when Lissa rushed out of the kitchen nearly twelve hours earlier. The frightened look on her face prompted him to conduct his own search in the immediate vicinity by going door-to-door to see if anyone had seen the child. He attempted to call Lissa later that evening. When he couldn't reach her, he reported the incident to the police.

"We may have been responsible for her, Jan, but it wasn't our fault." He gently laid his hand on her shoulder. "We did what we could."

Jay recalled how fervently he tried to call Lissa but couldn't leave a message. Voicemail was full. *And how do I tell her what Becca confessed? That's a message no mother wants to hear.*

****

Hellinger? Lissa studied the name. A sinking feeling came over her. "Detective, do you know anything about the Hellingers? Their history?"

He looked at her askance and shook his head. "It's not ringing a bell," he said with a frown. "But—"

"*I* do. You see, my father was an attorney. We lived here in Pinewood when I was a kid. Just before my dad died—and the cause of his death was kind of sketchy, at best. My mother thought he was murdered—anyway, there was a guy named Joe Hellinger. He had some kind of drug cartel thing going on—"

"Yeah, I read about that," Brian interrupted. "Something about a million-dollar heist, wasn't it? Going on right under the cops' noses. I think Jessup's Diner was a front for it or something."

"What year was this?" the detective asked.

"In the late 70s," she said. "My dad put him away. Well, the judge did, but my dad was the leading attorney. My uncle told me about it. He had news clippings and everything."

The detective drew silent. He pulled out his notebook and scribbled something down.

"I don't know how—or if it's related to your daughter being missing—but let's go."

Detective Hastings led the way up to the house. The uneven walkway, having seen better days, appeared cracked in several spots, and the lawn was weedy and overgrown. The house itself in need of attention, too. The stone foundation was crumbling, and some of the shingles hung askew like skin attempting to shed itself. Lissa clutched Brian's arm for support as her own limbs were no stronger than rubber.

The detective glanced at his watch. "It's almost seven-thirty, still a bit early to be knocking but—"

A gruff voice called from across the yard. "Help ya?" An older man in work clothes stood holding a broom, his belly as big as a kettle.

"Yes, sir. I'm Detective Sergeant Hastings, Elmdale borough." The detective pulled out his ID and stepped toward him. "Just wanted a word with someone about the disappearance of Lacy Logan." He turned toward Lissa. "This is her mother."

Lissa stared at the man wondering if she knew him or was it just a sense of déjà vu? His dark hair hid most of his countenance, but something around the eyes reminded her of someone. She wanted to comb down the mangy beard he wore or—better still—take a pair of scissors to it.

"I, uh, don't know anything about it, sir."

"Are you the man of the house?" the detective asked, pulling out his notebook.

"Yes, yes, sir. I'm in charge, I guess. Since my daddy went away, anyways."

"Do you have a minute to talk?"

"Guessin' I do, sure."

"Your name?"

"Hellinger. Rob Hellinger."

"Mr. Hellinger, I'd like to ask you some questions inside if that's all right with you?"

Lissa froze. *Rob Hellinger*? *The paper boy*?

Chapter Twenty-Nine

"Yes?"

"Lissa? It's Aunt Celia. We heard about Lacy. Have they found her yet?"

The sound of her aunt's anxious voice sent Lissa's own emotions swaying. Now, she was sorry to have taken the call. Celia had already left a message the night before. She would have eventually returned the call, but she wanted to tell them in her own time, not now while she stood in the Hellinger's house.

"No, Aunt Celia. Not yet." Her voice just over a whisper.

"Oh, Lissa, how awful."

"Listen, I can't talk right now. I'll call you back when—"

"Lissa," she interrupted. "Your uncle wants to come out there—to help. It was my idea that we both come out but he wants to do it alone. You know your uncle…when he gets a notion about something, he's—"

"But I'm not home right now, Aunt Celia. I'll call you after I'm—"

"Are you all right, dear? Is anyone with you?"

"I'm with Brian, and a detective from the police department. We're on a lead right now. We're at the Hellingers'."

"The Hellingers? You mean *The* Hellingers?"

Once Lissa opened her mouth, she realized she'd

said too much. Her lack of sleep and intense anxiety left little in the way of discretion. With the cotton in her head, her decision-making skills at this point floundered.

"I—I guess so." She glanced around the entryway where she took the call, keeping an eye on Brian and the detective in the living room.

"Where are they? What's the address?"

"It's in my neighborhood. Veronica Street. I have to go now. I'll call you back soon, okay?" She heard a click. "Aunt Celia?" She hung up the phone wondering if the call disconnected, or if Aunt Celia abruptly hung up and rushed to tell Uncle Charlie. *Please God, don't let him get involved.*

Was she really standing in the home of Rob Hellinger, the same person she knew from the neighborhood when he was the newspaper boy? The neighborhood bully? Wouldn't it be just the kind of thing for his kin to be involved in something like the disappearance of a little girl? Now it all made sense.

He'd been rough, even for a little boy. She remembered the time when he bullied little Donny. When the poor kid became visibly upset, Lissa helplessly stood watching. It broke her heart. Calling out one of the Hellingers might have gotten him even more riled. The whole community—at least those she knew—seemed wary of the Hellingers as though they were a contagion, of sorts; the details, though, had never been explained fully to her. Apparently, the Hellingers were not ones to contend with. She could barely hold herself together with all the impulses racing through her head.

Inside the next room, Brian stood next to the

detective in the living room. A dingy green paisley print sofa, two matching Queen Anne chairs, and a couple of pine end tables were arranged on the worn hardwood floor. The walls, painted a yellowy eggshell, bore water stains on the ceiling. In the corner, an old Baldwin piano. A musty smell of old firewood and dampness hung in the air. As if the room weren't creepy enough, Lissa spotted a centipede on the wall that totally grossed her out.

"So who owns the yellow car?" Detective Hastings asked, turning a page in his notebook.

"It's Kyle's," he replied as though it was common knowledge. "My nephew."

"Is he around? I'd like to talk with him."

"What's he done?" the man demanded.

"That's what I'd like to talk to him about."

Rob Hellinger clenched and unclenched his fists. "He do something?"

"Didn't say he did." The detective's tone remained calm and measured. "Mr. Hellinger, no one is casting any aspersions here. We just need to speak with him."

The man turned and took a step back. "Sis," the man called into the next room. His voice gurgled with phlegm. "Connie, where's Kyle?"

A woman in a pink quilted robe pattered into the room, her straw-toned hair wrapped up under a black headband. "I thought I heard voices," she said, startled at the sight of them. "Oh, dear." Her eyes darted back and forth while she pulled the robe's lapels in tighter across her chest. "What's happened?"

"This here's Detective, uh Detective—"

"Hastings," the detective interjected, flashing his credentials.

"They wanna talk to Kyle. He up yet or did he leave for school?"

"He's..." Her eyes glanced up toward the ceiling. "...upstairs."

"We're here to investigate the disappearance of a little girl named Lacy Logan," the detective said.

"Oh, dear."

"And what is your relation to Kyle?"

"Kyle?" Her eyes enlarged. "I'm his mother."

"We just want to speak to him briefly, ma'am. If you could—"

"He took my daughter!" Lissa broke out in a half-scream and lunged toward her. "That's what he's *done*." Brian pulled her back by the arm. "He picked her up last night—Halloween night—in his car," she yelled. The adrenaline coursing through her veins gave her a boldness she didn't know she possessed.

The woman slowly shook her head as Lissa barked, "There's a witness who saw the whole thing. I've spoken to her. Now where is he?"

The woman clutched her neck. "Oh, no, dear, you must be mistaken."

A rush of heat, like fire, rose up inside Lissa. "A lady said she saw my daughter get into a *yellow* car." She extended her arm toward the direction of the driveway. "Just like the one parked outside. Are you telling me that there's more than one mustard yellow car in this county?" Spit flew out of her mouth.

A young man appeared from around the corner dressed in jeans and an untucked flannel shirt. The woman turned to him and reached out to grasp his arm. "Kyle, these people are...this woman, well, she thinks you—"

"Kidnapped." Lissa broke in to finish the woman's sentence. "Where's my daughter? What have you done with Lacy?"

The teen looked aghast. "Your daughter? I didn't kidnap nobody."

"My daughter is missing since last night—twelve hours ago." She tapped her wrist indicating the time although she didn't wear a watch.

Detective Hastings pulled back his shoulders and faced the teen. "Son, we have reason to believe Ms. Logan's daughter may have gotten into a yellow car sometime Halloween night. That's when she was last seen by anyone. Are you saying you don't know anything about it?"

The teen crossed his arms across his chest. "No, sir, I don't," he said boldly.

"Then where were you last night between five and eight o'clock?" Lissa demanded.

"He was right here," Connie retorted with an exaggerated nod and pointed to the floor. "Right here at home."

"Can you vouch for that Mr. Hellinger?" the detective asked.

"Most certainly can."

"You're sure?"

"Sure as shootin', I am."

"Mr. Detective sir," Connie began. "My son was not out last night. He stopped trick-or-treating years ago, and there would be no reason he would be out."

"I'm not implying he was trick-or-treating, ma'am, I'm inquiring whether he was out in his car." The detective nodded toward the window. "That your car— the yellow one outside?"

"Yes, sir, it's mine," Kyle said.

"Were you out last night cruising—or something—in your car?"

"No, sir, I wasn't."

"Can you prove that?"

"Yes, sir, I can."

The detective cocked his head. "How's that, son?"

"Got a dead battery, sir. I haven't driven her in over a week."

Chapter Thirty

"Now what?" Lissa questioned the detective after leaving the house. Totally crushed, she felt the blunt force of hitting a stone wall at the boy's statement.

"We don't give up, that's what. Between Crimestoppers, the Amber Alert, and multiple police districts involved, we'll find your daughter, Ms. Logan."

"Do you believe him?" she asked.

"The kid?" He turned to glance back at the house. "Yeah, I do. I mean he's rough around the edges, but that clunker of a car looks like it could barely run itself into the ground." The detective reached for his ringing phone.

Brian pulled Lissa into his arms. "It's *you* who needs to believe right now." Brian's blue eyes softened. They held a measure of love and sympathy that made her want to cry. "We'll find her, Liss." He held her until the detective got off the phone.

In a moment of clarity, the haunting image of the SUV from back in the summer came to her.

"Wait," she began, excitedly. Brian let go of her, and she turned to face the detective. "There's something I forgot—" She paused. "It probably wasn't anything, really. But a while back we were tailed by someone on the road."

"You and your daughter?" Detective Hastings

asked, reaching for his notebook.

She nodded. "A white SUV."

"You sure about that, Liss?" Brian questioned, his brow furrowing.

"Positive," she said with a nod.

The detective kept his gaze on Lissa. "I'm listening," he said intently.

"We were driving back from Lacy's school. All through the city on the way home it followed right behind; that is, until I pulled up to a police station. Then it hightailed out of there."

"Was it a man or woman at the wheel?" he asked.

Lissa shook her head. "I don't know for sure. I couldn't tell."

Brian's face closed in. "You never told me about that," he said.

She shrugged. "I didn't want to burden you with my problems." *I didn't want to scare you away.*

The detective wrote something down in his notebook. "Anything else?"

Lissa looked first at Brian and then back to the detective. "I already told the first responding officer everything I could think of…I thought that info would be related to the Peeping Tom…and the neighbor. You don't think any of this is related, do you?"

"Every town has a Peeping Tom," said the detective. "I'm not sure what we can do about them unless they're caught in the act." He paused. "Now what about the neighbor?"

"Just a guy who lives in the neighborhood. He was outside my window one day. I'm sure he's fine." She rolled her eyes. "I was just being paranoid." She paused. "And we had a break-in, too. Back in the early summer…nothing stolen or anything."

The detective continued writing. "Nothing was stolen, you say?"

She shook her head. "Nothing I'm aware of." She paused. "But I reported it to the police just the same."

"Okay, so back to the neighbor. What's the name?"

"Mike. Mike Hemstead."

"So what happened?"

"Well, it's just a hunch, and it's probably nothing, just odd."

"And?" the detective interjected.

"He was outside my window working one day during the summer."

"This is odd…how?" he asked.

"He said he was working on the air conditioning, but, oh, well, it's probably nothing."

"No, no, go on," he said impatiently.

"Well, his tool belt—"

"Tool belt? What about it, Ms. Logan?"

"It was brand new." She paused. "If a maintenance worker has been around, wouldn't his tool belt look— well…wouldn't it be worn?"

The detective stared into the distance as though in a trance. He closed his notebook and said, "You may have something there, Ms. Logan. I'm impressed."

Don't flatter me, sir. Please just find my daughter.

The crisp, November air whisked through the trees, scattering leaves carelessly across the streets and sidewalks. November was always dreary. Her mother went home to be with the Lord last year at this time, and it was the first month of the fall season where the weather often turned bleak. She hated November and wished the calendar skipped from October to the New

Year. January was bleak, too. But, at least, the days were longer and springtime on the horizon. *What good can come in November?* She knew of too many instances where these kinds of situations turned out for the worst. Whether in true-to-life stories or movies, the happy ending wasn't always within reach. Sometimes, evil in this world happened and, sadly, the innocent suffered. She wanted to shuck the thoughts from her mind, hoping they would scatter away like crisp leaves in the wind.

Lissa glanced back at the house hoping for a sign they'd been right all along, and Rob Hellinger's nephew was indeed culpable in Lacy's disappearance. She searched the windows to see if someone inside possibly had regrets about their story and stood staring out with guilt in their eyes. The windows remained closed, the shades drawn. Like blind eyes.

Who else could it have been? Her thoughts raced. Though, oddly, her emotions remained calm. There were no tears. Not like last night where they flowed for hours. From somewhere deep inside, a quiet peace came over her. God doesn't give anything we can't handle, she knew. She prayed silently that God would ordain her next steps.

"Okay, well, it looks like we've got another lead," the detective said, putting his phone back in his breast pocket. "I'm going to drop you off back at your house, Ms. Logan, 'cause I have a full day. But I'll be in touch, so stay close to your phone."

"What kind of lead?" she asked.

"I'm not sure right now. That's what I have to go find out."

Chapter Thirty-One

Woodward's department store hummed with afternoon shoppers. New Thanksgiving displays replaced old Halloween decorations and featured "hot ticket" signs on the backs of paper turkeys at strategic eye-level spots all over the store. Sales associate Jennifer Duncan in the Junior's department busily rang up a short queue of customers as Bill Cummings from security made his rounds. In between customers, he caught her eye, giving her a subtle nod that everything was under control in the area. Normally, he made his rounds unannounced, slipping through the aisles of display racks without much fanfare. Dressed in street clothes, no one was the wiser of his security detail: a detective exclusively hired to spot pilferers. With the extra customers in the store, his radar was primed.

Women, young and old, stepped into and out of the dressing rooms. The pattern seemed pretty routine for the first hour on duty until something caught his eye. A slim, petite brunette walked into the dressing room with a white scoop neck top underneath a denim jacket. She carried a stack of items on hangers in with her; however, on her return, it appeared the top she now wore looked different to him. A yellow top appeared from under a denim jacket and her torn jeans looked much tighter than before. The detective kept an eye on her while she lingered, casually exploring the

171

department, and fondling the merchandise. She ambled across the wide marble floor toward the lingerie department and paused at the display where slips, bras, and assorted silky items in pastel colors were marked down to half-price. When the young girl maneuvered around the table, the detective caught sight of something underneath her denim jacket. A dangling price tag.

"Excuse me, miss. Just wondering if you were going to pay for those items you have there."

The girl innocently looked up at him. With a dumbfounded expression she said, "These?" She held up a pair of leopard-print underwear. "Oh, I'm just looking today."

Detective Cummings said, "How about the clothes underneath your jacket? Are you just looking at those, too?"

Chapter Thirty-Two

"That's my brother," Officer Dwayne McCall said with astonishment when he scanned the accident in the log. The report included emergency response from neighboring Carroll and Washington counties, and a medical helicopter was called to the scene. He remembered it well. The sight of the crumpled hunk of metal that was once a vehicle turned his stomach upside down. "When did this come in, Rachel?"

"Not long ago. Sometime late last night," the secretary said. "Why?"

Officer McCall didn't have time to respond and was out of the building and on the phone in his patrol car within seconds. There was only one hospital he knew with a landing pad. A call to the hospital's main desk confirmed his younger brother had been admitted last night and was in room 402. By the seventh unanswered ring to his private phone, he disconnected and called the hospital back to request the nurse's station to inquire about his brother. The nurse on duty told him he'd been called down to x-ray. "He'll need some clothes," she added. "It would be helpful if someone brought some along with other essentials, if possible, to the hospital."

"Oh, sure. I'll swing by his place," Dwayne replied, grateful that his brother was still alive. "I'll bring everything he needs."

"How's it going?" fellow officer Gerry Seitz called out the window, pulling into the adjacent parking space.

"Hey, Ger," he said, pokerfaced.

"You look like the world just fell on top of you. Y'all right?"

"I just found out my brother was in a car accident."

"Too bad. Which accident?"

"The one on I-340 last night."

"Heard about it. Pretty bad. Was it a full moon or something? Heard the highway was shut down for hours."

"Yep."

"So how's he doing?"

"He's alive." He gave a weak smile. "That's about all I know. I'm going to his apartment now to get some of his things."

"I'll come with you," Gerry said. "I'm done for the day and my wife is away. Got nothing better to do."

****

The one-bedroom apartment sat amid a cluster of garden-style buildings nestled by a grove of shade trees on Queen's Chapel road. The last time he'd been here was the day he helped Don move in, close to a decade ago. Don insisted on giving him a key—just in case. Dwayne thought he didn't need to be a guardian to Don, not anymore. He'd been needy as a child, being smaller than most of the kids his age, and Dwayne often stood up for him when the occasional bully threatened him. They'd always been close and even more so after their parents passed away. When the opportunity came along for Don to get his own place to live, Dwayne was genuinely happy his little brother had the fortitude to step out on his own.

When he pulled up to the curb, an elderly woman standing on the sidewalk seemed alarmed at their presence.

"Anything the matter, officers?" she inquired, bearing a worried frown.

Dwayne tipped his hat to her and answered, "No, no, ma'am, we're just here on a friendly visit is all." He gave her his best smile, hoping to allay her fears.

Inside the quiet interior of the tiny vestibule, they stopped in front of the row of mailboxes where his brother's name was etched in handwritten ink at the top of A-2. They took the short set of stairs down to the lower floor with two gray doors and two more on each side of the hall. He searched for the key. A trace of latex paint hung in the air.

The bare bones apartment spoke to the practicality of bachelorhood. Leather chair. Television. Dining table. Dwayne went to Don's bedroom while Gerry waited in the living room. Upon opening the dresser, he found two pairs of jeans and several cotton pullovers and T-shirts. He gathered them along with several pairs of socks and all his underwear. Who knew how long he would be away from home. On top of the wood bureau among the clutter sat his asthma medication and an inhaler. Dwayne placed everything into a leftover grocery bag he found stashed in the lower cupboard of the kitchen.

On the way out, he noticed some papers strewn haphazardly on the dining room table along with some photos of nature scenes. He picked up one of them. In the corner of the room sat a folded-up tripod and a long-range telescope.

Chapter Thirty-Three

When Dwayne McCall stepped off the fourth-floor elevator of the Holy Cross Hospital, he braced himself. He didn't have a fear of blood or guts, but the unease filling him as he moved down the hall was palpable. In the overly bright fluorescent lights, patients were wheeled up and down the hallway on stretchers. The hospital personnel wore their best smiles when they passed. Whether it was the uniform or just their work ethic, he didn't know, but whenever he wore the blue, he felt more respected than any other time. He politely nodded on his way through the corridor, not knowing whether the patients were on their death beds or just in for maintenance repairs. Most of the injuries he witnessed as part of his job didn't affect him emotionally, but this time, a sick feeling formed in his stomach on the way to his brother's room.

"You doing all right, Mr. McCall?" the nurse asked and reached for the cord to draw the privacy curtain around his bed.

"Sore as a beat-up hound dog." His words came out slow and scratchy.

Dwayne didn't know how bad his brother's injury was, but judging by the damage to the vehicles, it was a miracle he was alive. The semi-private room held another patient dozing in the two-bed suite. A game show blared from the TV anchored in the ceiling.

The nurse pulled back the curtain surrounding his brother's bed and looked up to see Dwayne standing at the threshold. "Good morning, Officer," she said with a smile and beckoned him inside. "You have a visitor," she told Don and swiftly turned to leave.

"Hey," Dwayne said as he shuffled toward the bed. "Sorry about the accident, man."

Don spoke in a hoarse voice. "Yeah, nothing like getting up close and personal with a semi-tractor trailer."

"I'm sure." He chuckled. "You're lucky there were three cars in front of you. Can't say the same for some of them. At least two fatalities."

Don grunted and shook his head.

"I went to your place and got some clothes." He held up the bag of personal effects he picked up from Don's apartment. "Got your asthma medicine, too."

"Thanks, man. Just put it over there on the bureau. Did you bring the inhaler?"

"Yeah, it's all here, I think." He inspected the bag and, moments later, frowned. "Crap, where's the inhaler? Sorry, I thought I picked it up. I'll go back for it."

"Thanks, I'd appreciate it."

Dwayne studied the traction set-up where Don's leg hung motionless. He figured there was severe trauma to his body but was hesitant to inquire just how injurious the accident had been. The shock of seeing him in this condition rendered him dumb for the moment. Compared to his brother, he got the good end of the deal—house, wife, twin boys. Now poor Don got a raw deal—again. He eyed the elaborate mechanism of straps and pulleys and wondered if his brother would ever walk again.

The doctor came into the room and walked to his bedside. "I'm Doctor Hodgeson. Looks like you've gotten yourself into a bit of trouble I see," he said with a doctor's professional half-grin, attempting to lighten the situation. He glanced at Dwayne.

"Doctor," Dwayne nodded and extended his hand. "I'm his brother."

The doctor shook it and then plopped his hands on the railing around the bed. "You've been banged up pretty good there, Mr. McCall," he said and turned back to Dwayne as if speaking to him as well. "But you're going to be all right."

A wave of relief shot through Dwayne. "That's great news, doctor."

"Glad to hear it, Doc," Don echoed.

"But how long will he be in—in this condition?" Dwayne asked.

"In traction? Well, it'll be some time before we move him out of here. In some cases, the spinal compression fractures he's endured may end up being permanent injuries, but we're on a wait-and-see period before the final assessment. Then he'll be able to tell us himself whether he's got either weakness or complete numbness in his lower back." The doctor studied the report. "It's the L-3 and L-4 that I'm concerned with; otherwise, he's just got a broken leg and some minor bruises that will heal one-hundred percent, I'm certain." He tapped his pen on the paperwork.

"Then rehab?" Dwayne asked.

The doctor nodded. "Rehab is a given, yes. But I'm confident he'll do well."

Dr. Hodgeson made a few notes on the chart and

turned to leave.

"Thanks, Doctor," said Dwayne.

"Thank *you*," the doctor replied with a knowing look.

Dwayne knew the look. The doctor left the room and Dwayne focused on Don. Even more pressing than his brother's physical condition, there was something else on his mind he needed to discuss with him. He knew this wasn't the best place or the perfect time to discuss family business, but the concern he bore for his brother weighed more than convenience.

Dwayne picked up the TV remote and turned the sound to mute. "I hope you don't mind, Donny, I just want to talk for a moment. A lull came over the room, and Dwayne bit his lip before speaking. "You up for talking?"

"Sure, I'm sore, but I can still talk. What's on your mind?"

Dwayne paused and gathered his courage. "The telescope I saw at your apartment…you know, when I was over there this morning getting your stuff."

His mind floated back to the dining room table where pictures lay. "Does it still work?"

With a quizzical look, Don replied, "My telescope? Yeah, why?"

"Just wondered what you used it for."

Silence.

Dwayne quickly looked away not wanting to appear too obvious in what he was asking. During last week's staff meeting, the one community issue stuck out in his mind was the Peeping Tom report with another citing in the area. Officer Matthews said there were two recent reports of a man with a baseball cap who was seen lingering in the woods by Glenwood Swim Club. Dwayne didn't think his brother was the Peeping Tom, but he did have a fetish for baseball caps. Don wasn't the type, Dwayne tried to convince himself. He believed his brother wouldn't be capable of anything unseemly. Not until he noticed the picture on his brother's table. The picture of the little girl.

"Why do you ask?"

"Nothing in particular. Just wondering."

"I—I like to look at stuff, you know, up close. It's been a hobby of mine for a while. Actually, I have a camera, too, that I use on occasion. You know, when something special pops into the lens."

Dwayne opened the bag where he stashed Don's things and pulled out the picture. "Donny, do you know this little girl?"

Don squinted at the 5 x 7 color photograph.

"Well?" Dwayne said impatiently.

"Yeah, I know her."

"How do you know her?" He struggled not to sound like an interrogator.

"I took the picture."

Chapter Thirty-Four

Detective Hastings had a pile of messages waiting on his desk when he got to his office. Stacks of reports and miscellaneous paperwork collected in neat piles taking up all four corners. Among the papers sat a jar of pickled eggs. He rifled through the messages and made a few phone calls before his assistant, Dorinda Walcott, stuck her head in.

"Did you get my message?" she asked, eyeing his cluttered desk from the doorway. "I put it right by the phone."

Puzzled, he searched through the pink slips of paper. "I've got a swamp load here."

"It should be on top, sir. Red ink."

With his cigarette dangling from his lips, Detective Hastings rifled through the messages again. "This? When did this come in?"

"This morning, sir."

"Why didn't someone call me?" he barked.

"We tried to notify you but there was no answer and your voice mailbox was full. Sergeant Matthews brought it over."

He shook his head and picked up the phone. "Thanks, Dor, didn't mean to get upset with you."

"Understood, sir," she said turning to leave. "Oh, any word on the street about the little girl?"

Now on the phone, he raised his free hand in the

air. "From my lips to God's ears. I'm on it now. Yeah, hey, Marty? Yeah, hold on a minute." He cupped the phone. "Do you mind getting me a coffee, Dor? Black with two sugars?"

"Certainly, sir."

"Oh, and what is this?" he asked, pointing to the jar.

Dorinda grinned. "Oh, Mrs. Jennings brought that in," she explained. The detective turned up his nose. "Just a thank you gift for getting her dog out of the well." She put her hand on her hip. "Everyone got one, even the deputy."

"Got it." He frowned. "Better take it away, though. I think I'm allergic to eggs—at least, pickled purple ones." He waved his hand in front of the jar in a shooing gesture.

"Yes, sir," she said, promptly reaching over to remove the jar.

"Marty, sorry about that. So you're sure it's the Maryland girl?" Detective Hastings said. "How old?"

"Not sure, but she matches the description on the Amber Alert."

"Why are we hearing about it now?" he asked. "Is this the same one you gave me earlier? I couldn't make out your words there toward the end."

"The alert didn't hit West Virginia."

"West Virginia?" He sat up. "You're saying she's in West Virginia?"

"Seems so unless there's more than one missing. It's gotta be the same girl."

"What's her condition… dead or alive?"

"Hopefully, still alive."

"Still? What's going on?"

"She's been admitted to Jefferson Medical Center in Ranson, West Virginia."

"Okay, tell Matthews I'm on it. Leaving now."

Detective Hastings hung up and redialed.

"Hello?"

"Mrs. Logan. Detective Hastings. We have a lead, and it's looking significant."

"Significant? What's that mean?" Her spirit lightened.

"I think we found your daughter."

****

Detective Hastings knew he made a mistake in getting personally involved in the missing girl case yet telling someone there was a chance their daughter was alive and witnessing their joy was the best part of his detective work. Being a small-town detective, it was hard not to get involved. The folks in the community became like family over the years, and word in the department was that Lissa's father, a prominent attorney, had busted one of the biggest drug cartels in the state. The capture was the biggest coup in the county. From then on, John Leads became a major figure around town and his name carried a lot of weight. Taking care of the townspeople, especially John Leads' girl, was not only his solemn obligation but his heartfelt duty as well.

In the past, he was wrong only once when the discovery of the lost boy in the woods turned out bad. Very bad. In his twenty years of service that was the only time he felt like he failed. He stubbed out his cigarette and rolled the window down to let some fresh air in at the approach to Bellevue Avenue, hoping this would not be a repeat of that heartbreaking case.

Chapter Thirty-Five

Lissa could barely contain the cascade of emotions coursing through her. The good word from the detective about Lacy sent her over the moon, though the concern over why she was in the hospital struck like a hammer.

"Here comes a dark SUV," she said anxiously. "Is that him?"

"Looks like it," Brian said as the vehicle slowed with the detective behind the wheel. He lifted his hand in the air as though hailing a taxi as the SUV pulled to the curb. When it came to a stop, Brian opened the back door.

The smell of old cigarette smoke assaulted her nose as she hopped in. Though, Lissa didn't mind. The interior could have reeked of a cesspool for all she cared. The odor paled in comparison to the gratitude she bore for Detective Hasting's assistance.

"I can't tell you how excited I am right now, Detective," she said, hopping into the back seat with Brian right behind her. Still, she could not bring herself to calling him *Hal*. "But how did she end up in West Virginia? It's miles away."

"Don't know. We're not even sure it's your daughter…just a lead, Mrs. Logan." Her heart sank. "But it's a promising one," he said. "We'll soon see."

"You said it was Jefferson Memorial?" she asked.

"That's what they reported."

"Where is that? Just over the border from Maryland?"

"GPS tells me it's less than twenty miles right across the bridge. In Ranson."

"I better call Aunt Celia and Uncle Charlie." Lissa pulled out her phone. "They'll want to know."

In her overly excited state, Lissa dialed the number wrong twice before she got it right. She could barely hold the phone without shaking.

"Hello?"

"Aunt Celia? Hi, it's me."

"Any word yet on Lacy?" she asked, anxiously. "Your uncle and I are on the edge of our seats. He wants to come out there, but I told him to wait for your call."

"That's what I'm calling about. The authorities think they know where she is."

"Hallelujah," she screamed. "That's wonderful, where is she?"

"In Ranson. Ranson, West Virginia. She's—"

"A ransom? They're asking for a ransom for her? Oh, dear Lord."

"No, no, Aunt Celia, that's the name of the town."

"How much?"

"There's *no* ransom. I said *Ranson*, as in Ranson, West Virginia."

"No ransom?"

"No, no ransom. She's in the hospital. Listen, you're fading in and out. Let me call you back when we get to the hospital. If you want, you can you can meet us there. It's not far from you. It's Jefferson Memorial Children's Hospital."

Mid-day traffic was relatively light along I-340 on

the ride into West Virginia as the vehicle sped down the highway. Lissa chewed the inside of her lips, mentally playing every possible scenario of what could be soon facing her at the hospital. Would it be Lacy? Would she be in a coma or just shaken from an accident or worse—would it be just another eight-year-old girl with similar features? It wouldn't be the first time identities got mixed up. Even going as far as thinking one's child was still alive but soon coming to know their child died...it was a twin look-alike who survived a tragic accident...their hopes now capsized in vain.

The crisp fall air smelled sweet coming through the partially open window up front, and Lissa snuggled closer to Brian to steer clear of the cold draft. He placed his hand on top of hers, and he looked her in the eye with an expression that said: *Either way, this is going to be all right.* Though she was nervous at the prospects before her, his demeanor calmed her. Without any confidence of her own, she felt secure in his. The rich, musky suede scent of his cologne reminded her of the other men in her life who'd loved her. She hoped Brian did, too.

The drive along this stretch of I-340 took her back to the times Uncle Charlie drove them this way to the country through the fields and farmland of western Maryland on the way across the river to Harpers Ferry. Only now she was no longer the little girl without a care in the world asking every few miles, *"Are we there yet?"*

Puffy gray-bottom clouds shifted across the sapphire blue sky intermittently obscuring the sun. The last billboard before entering West Virginia featured a secluded B&B. "The best of old world hospitality plus all the comforts of home." Lissa never noticed the invitation. The sign swiftly passed in a blur. Her mind couldn't register the words. Although the scenery reflected the beauty of calendar pictures—trees painted bright crimson and gold on a backdrop of mountain peaks and river gorges—she barely took note of any of it. The scenery may as well have been in black and white. Her anxious thoughts about Lacy cast a pall over everything.

The sound of crinkling paper caught her attention as Brian opened the bag he'd brought with him. "I know you're probably not hungry, but you need to eat something." He peeled back the plastic wrapping on a cream cheese bagel and took it apart, handing her half. She shook her head. "How about some coffee?" He placed a coffee stirrer into the hole in the top of the lid. She took the cup and held it in her palms. It wasn't steaming hot but warm enough to take the chill from her hands.

Before crossing the Shenandoah and Potomac rivers into West Virginia, she spotted a cider stand set among a copse of half-bare trees settled among a carpet of orange-colored leaves. Under normal conditions, she'd want to stop to enjoy the scenery and grab a cup, but today was not a time for leisurely pursuits. In fact, she wished he'd drive faster.

"Should be coming up on it soon," the detective announced.

Lissa's stomach knotted up again. Spotting the first glimpse of the red brick hospital in the distance, her heart skipped. She gazed at the four-story building and all but practically willed her daughter to be there. *Please, Lord, let it be Lacy…let it be my little girl.*

Detective Hastings turned into the parking garage and pulled into a spot on the second floor in section D. They took the stairway down one flight and headed for the main lobby. The massive glass pavilion loomed in the distance, and to Lissa, it was as though she were marching to her death. They met an elderly woman at the information desk. Detective Hastings did the talking, and the woman directed them to the third floor.

Lissa's heart beat wildly in the silence of the elevator. Brian slipped his arm around her as she leaned back against the handrail for support. She hadn't bathed in over 24 hours and was self-conscious about it, hoping no one else noticed. Detective Hastings, in his raincoat, maintained a serious expression. He held his gaze toward the elevator floor. A furrow creased his forehead. No one said a word until the polite ding of the elevator signaled their arrival.

"After you," the detective said, holding back the door for them to pass.

The sharp odor of ammonia and latex permeated the third floor where the children's unit buzzed with personnel making their way along the narrow hallway. They turned right at the "T" and followed the signs to room 307. Passing by the patients in room after room, the sight of the bedridden tucked under mounds of white bedding with only their heads visible echoed down the corridor. Lissa never felt comfortable in the sterile environment of a hospital with its stark whiteness and overly bright fluorescence. She gripped Brian's hand, now moist with perspiration. Or was it hers? After passing several rooms, a sudden fear pressed in on her. If Lacy wasn't in the hospital, what would be the odds of her being found at all?

"I'm frightened," she said in a half-sob, raising her hand to her mouth. "What if she's—"

"Shhh, don't go there, Liss." Brian pulled her aside and wrapped his arms around her. "Just breathe, Liss. Just breathe." He planted a gentle kiss on her lips.

Detective Hastings moved farther down the hall and stopped in front of room 307. Lissa took a deep breath. The fear of not recognizing her daughter—or worse, it not being her daughter—loomed. She clenched her teeth and took a step inside.

****

"That's my little friend." Don held the picture for a moment and then handed it back to Dwayne.

"Your friend?" Dwayne lent a quizzical look at his brother.

"Yep." He chuckled. "Well, not my best friend. She's just a kid."

"She a neighbor or…?"

"I met her in the woods when she was walking her dog. She wandered over one day when I was taking pictures. I was adjusting the telescope and she started asking me questions…that sort of thing. Then she told me about some treasure trove she found. Kids, gotta love 'em."

Dwayne listened to his brother as thoughts kept circling through his mind. *Was his brother the Peeping Tom?* The staff was told to pull out all the stops in finding the guy. His boss gave them heat to find him—and find him now. If it's one thing Sergeant Matthews hated was a Peeping Tom. No one ventured to ask why his face flushed beet red in anger when he spoke about it. Rumor had it there were personal reasons for the sergeant's voracious appetite to nail the guy. The department spurred into action as quickly as they could.

"So what's her name?"

Don paused for a moment and then shook his head. "You know, off the top of my head, I couldn't tell ya."

Chapter Thirty-Six

Lissa bolted into the room and flew to her daughter's bedside. The child lay under the sheets with a white bandage wound around her head.

"Lacy!" she cried. A flood of joy rained through every sinew in her body, setting off a billow of tears. She flung herself across the bed and wrapped her body around the tiny bundle under the covers.

Lacy opened her eyes and looked up at her mother, expressionless. "Mom." Her voice came out just above a whisper.

Lissa held her daughter's face and kissed the bandage on her forehead. "I'm so glad to see you, baby." She wiped her eyes. *You have no idea.* She proceeded to pepper the child with questions: "Are you in any pain? How did you get into the accident? Was someone driving you home?" Then she saw Lacy's listless eyes opening and closing and realized in her medicated state, she wasn't able to process the questions.

"She might be in shock," Brian said in a heavy whisper.

"I wish I could talk to her nurse," Lissa said and turned toward the door, hoping for one of the aids to step inside. "Or even better, the doctor."

Brian put his hand on her shoulder and said, "I'll go see if I can find someone."

Lissa caught the eye of the detective, who stood by the door. She got up off the bed. "Detective, how can I thank you?"

Detective Hastings stood with his hands in his pockets and shrugged. "It was a team effort, Ms. Logan."

Lissa hugged him, and her vision clouded with fresh tears.

****

"She has a grade two concussion with some contusions," the doctor said. "We gave her a CT scan and some mild pain relievers."

"Is she in shock?" Lissa asked, worriedly chewing her lip.

"Yes, when she was first brought in, we noticed the initial signs—dizziness and such, but it should wane over the next few hours. It may linger for more than that, but in my experience, children are much more adaptable than adults when it comes to things like this," the doctor said, his eyes focused on her. "Of course, this doesn't preclude keeping an eye out for any negative changes."

"Like what?"

The doctor's countenance remained stoic. "Mood swings, anger, or the inability to get along with other children…that kind of thing."

"It looks like all she wants to do is sleep. Is that okay?" Lissa asked.

"Sleep is actually going to make her brain recover," the doctor said. "We've been monitoring her and waking her every couple of hours to make sure everything is progressing the way it should. Her scan revealed nothing out of the ordinary in my opinion. No hydrocephalus, no serious damage. She is very fortunate."

Lacy stirred for a moment. "Mom," she said weakly. "I was in an accident."

"Yes, baby, I know. I've been frantic with worry, we all have—Aunt Celia and Uncle Charlie and Brian." She looked at Brian and her heart melted. *What would I have done without you, Bri?* She turned back to Lacy. "Lacy, what happened? Why did you leave Becca's Halloween Party?"

Lacy's expression couldn't have been more pitiful to Lissa with her doleful green eyes peering up like a lost puppy. Her eyelids appeared heavy and in a matter of seconds, she fell back asleep.

Chapter Thirty-Seven

Dwayne McCall headed back to Don's apartment to retrieve the inhaler. He thought about the story his brother relayed to him involving the little girl and remained on the fence about reporting him as a possible Peeping Tom. How could he report his own brother? His conscience fought with him the whole way until the voice of Erlene Wilson from command broke in on the radio.

"Radio to Two-twenty."

"Two-twenty."

"Assistance needed at Queen's Park Plaza apartments. Building B."

"Copy that."

What's going on at Don's apartment building?

When Dwayne pulled up in front of building B, two other police cars, flashers on, were already parked. He flung open the door and ran across the lawn toward the building.

"What's going on?" Dwayne asked colleague Cliff Gilson, who stood at the outside door.

"Hey, Dwayne," he replied. "Got a report on the Peeping Tom."

"Peeping Tom?"

"Yeah, we're going in."

"What are you going in for? You got a search warrant?"

"Yep."

"What for?"

"A telescope."

The apartment superintendent stood at the front door to Don's apartment holding a large ring of keys. Dwayne knew the authorities smelled something afoul with his brother. However circumstantial the evidence of a telescope was, there would be no certifiable evidence of anything without the pictures. *Or the negatives. Were there negatives? Where was the camera?* Dwayne tensed at the scene in front of him.

"Here it is," said the superintendent in a thick middle-eastern accent as the correct key finally fit. He opened the door.

Two officers, Frank Myers and Joe Tremont, led the way inside. Dwayne followed closely behind and tried to mentally assess the situation. How much trouble could his brother be in? For what could he possibly be held accountable? He had his own suspicions after seeing the telescope; though, instinctively, it just didn't add up. His brother was not a Peeping Tom.

Dwayne pulled Joe aside. "So what's the telescope prove? Anything?"

Joe looked at him squarely. "Peeping Tom. Intruder. It's a catalyst for other criminal behavior, you know that. Like weed can lead to heroin. I think the Sergeant is putting him or whoever it is together with the recent break-in on Bellevue. Said he thinks they could be the same person." He shrugged. "I don't know, but the Sarge says the guy's been followed back here a couple of times after being sighted in the woods."

Dwayne's heart sank when Frank lifted and tagged the telescope.

"Looks like this thing has a camera, too," Frank said.

"If it's attached, it's part of the telescope. We can take it," said Joe.

Dwayne pulled Joe aside. "Joe, I gotta tell ya something. This guy isn't who they think he is. This guy is my *brother*."

Joe eyed him. "You're kidding me."

"No, I'm not. I know my brother. He wouldn't hurt a fly."

Joe shrugged. "It'll all come out in the wash. We have orders to retrieve this evidence."

"Who gave you guys the tip off?"

"About what?"

"That there was a telescope in here."

Joe shrugged again. "I heard Seitz talking about it. Said he saw it himself."

Dwayne silently cursed himself for the whole thing. If he had come alone to pick up his brother's belongings, this never would have happened.

Chapter Thirty-Eight

"Somebody said…" Lacy's words came out slowly "…I was adopted."

Lissa swallowed hard. She stood and walked toward the window, wishing she could keep walking, but then thought better of it. She'd never leave her precious daughter's side—not for a very long time. She turned toward Lacy. "Is that why you left the party…because someone said you were adopted?"

"And other stuff," she mumbled into the pillow.

"What, Lacy?" Lissa's voice turned soft.

"Some of the kids and Becca, too…they were laughing. And that mean girl was there."

"Mean girl?"

"The one who tried to cut me off coming home from school. She's Becca's cousin."

Lissa glanced at the detective who was taking notes. He nodded at her to continue.

The incident with the girl came back in a flash. Lissa wanted to speak to the girl's parents back then, but there was no way of knowing her name. Now she might have the chance to do just that.

"Was I…adopted?"

Lissa's pulse raced. She swallowed again, dreading the question. Several times in the past she pictured in her mind's eye the scenario of having to explain Lacy's background to her and the history of her adoption. She imagined telling her child the unvarnished version of what happened. Much of it paralleled the real-life task of when she explained to Lacy the facts of life when she was just six. This time, Lissa knew it would be different. The story would be personal; its impact, visceral.

Now, Lissa imagined the distinct opposite reaction from Lacy than the time she shared the facts of life with her over dinner at a quiet table in the corner of Sizzler's steakhouse. Lissa's imagination flashed with the possibility of Lacy quickly dissolving into tears at the realization she was not her biological child. Witnessing Lacy's hurt would drive a stake into Lissa's heart. She always dreaded the day when she would actually have to tell her child the harsh truth.

Lissa moved away from the window and sat on the edge of Lacy's bed. She wanted to share the back story of her life with Lacy for so long, but there was always something holding her back. The timing was never right. First, when her beloved sweetheart, Jason, had been a casualty of war at thirty years old, killed in the line of duty, the stress became so overwhelming it was all she could do to keep putting one foot in front of the other. Lacy wasn't even old enough for school. To shatter her innocence with something she possibly couldn't comprehend made Lissa reticent to even broach the subject. *In due time* she repeated to herself until the years passed, one-by-one. Now her daughter wanted to know and approached *her* on the topic. She wanted to crawl into a hole. The embarrassment for Lacy had been all her fault. How could she make this right for her daughter?

"Lacy, I need to tell you something. It's something

that I should have told you a long time ago. I wanted to. I really did. But—but there was so much going on—all too quickly—and, well…" She paused to think how much she was getting through to the child, who focused on her with barely an eye, sometimes closing it with the rest of her face pressed into the pillow. In mid-sentence Lissa's throat went dry as though she were performing on stage and had an unexpected case of stage fright. "I need to tell you—" she choked and then let out a series of dry coughs. Without any immediate relief, she got up and searched her purse for a lozenge. Finding an old Hall's cough drop at the bottom of her purse, she wiped if off with a fresh tissue and popped it into her mouth before sharing the story from nearly ten years ago…

~1996~

"Liss? Hi, it's me." Before Lissa could say anything, her cousin announced, "Guess what? I'm pregnant."

"You're…wait, what? Really?"

"Uh huh. The doctor just confirmed it."

"That's great news, Maria."

"Not really." Her words fell flat.

"Why?" Lissa asked, perplexed by her cousin's lack of enthusiasm.

"Let me put it this way. I'll probably be raising the baby on my own."

Shocked with the blunt pronouncement, Lissa tried to make sense of it. Her cousin had dated Hank Maloney since high school. Everyone assumed once he settled down, he'd marry Maria. Hank couldn't seem to find steady work for long and if he did, somehow, he always managed to get fired. Her relationship with him over the past nine years ran like an on again, off again cycle. After all this time, no one in the family understood why they weren't yet married—or even engaged. Lissa felt the burden her favorite cousin bore, if only vicariously, and wished for both of them that things could be different. Being married, Lissa desperately wanted a child, and now her cousin, unmarried and alone, was going to be a mother.

"So what's going on with Hank? Have you told him?"

"No, I haven't told anyone yet."

"What do you think he'll say?"

"Hank, *pffft*. He's not the kind of man who even wants to be married. He'd probably make an even worse father."

She ached for Maria, who always managed to pick the wrong man. Now approaching thirty, she held on fast to the only man that paid her any attention. Lissa kept her envy at bay. Yet she couldn't quite fathom how she and her husband, Jason, couldn't conceive while her out-of-wedlock cousin now found herself with child. What was God thinking?

As the months went by, Lissa did everything she could to help her closest cousin. With her Aunt Celia's recovery from knee surgery slowing her down, Lissa stepped in to help, and with Jason on another tour of duty, she had the time to invest. Between occasional errands, shopping, cleaning, taking care of organizing her baby shower including registering at the Babies "R" Us store and being a general right-hand gal, Lissa would have the opportunity to bond with not only her cousin but the new baby as well.

By the eighth month of her pregnancy, Maria began to feel sharp pains in her abdomen. A visit to the doctor led to a diagnosis of a disorder that included high blood pressure, and several tests indicated too much protein was in her body and neither enough calcium or magnesium. A diagnosis of preeclampsia came and soon led to more serious complications. Within a week, she was rushed to the hospital for a preterm delivery via Caesarian section.

Lissa and her mother, Anne, drove together to the hospital where the family convened. They anxiously waited for the baby's birth; the time couldn't go by fast enough. It seemed the hands on the wall clock were fueled by molasses.

"Where's Hank?" Lissa said, staring out the window. Three stories up from the main entrance, she had a clear view of the hospital parking area and the long curving driveway that led into the complex. The sun began to set, leaving a long shadow on the adjacent grass hill. "There's still no sign of him."

"Frankly, I don't think there will be," her Aunt Celia said with a sigh.

Her sweet, diminutive aunt held a distant look of pain in her eyes that told enough of the story. She didn't understand him and neither did anyone else.

"I told her from the start he was no good." She shook her head. "But getting through to Maria is impossible sometimes. Charlie and I both tried." She threw her arms into the air. "He's a bum. I don't know what she sees in him."

A stab thrust into her gut as if it were her own life hanging in the balance of an absentee father-to-be. *What's wrong with that guy? How awful for Maria.* She moved out of the waiting room to get a change of scenery and paced from one end of the bright fluorescent hallway to the other, hoping something would change by the time she returned. Hopefully, Hank would prove them all wrong and come running down the hall. Back and forth she went until the boredom of it all led her right back into the waiting room.

When she returned, a tall doctor in scrubs stood talking to them. His face bore a solemn expression. Maria died on the delivery table.

Chapter Thirty-Nine

Lissa watched Lacy shift under the covers. Her child was still struggling. Her whole world had done a one-eighty. Vulnerable to more onslaughts, she had to protect herself somehow—even to put some distance between them. Despite this, Lissa leaned closer to Lacy and laid a light hand on the pillow wedged between them, testing the waters of her closeness. "Are you hearing what I'm sharing with you, Lace?" Her words, soft and sweet.

A muffled reply came from behind the pillow, and Lissa took it as a *yes*. Lissa gently lowered the pillow and pulled it away from Lacy's face. Her mouth was set in a firm line, and her eyes were overly bright as though laced with tears that hadn't quite fallen. Lissa held her arms open and Lacy leaned into them.

"There, it's okay," Lissa said as Lacy sobbed. "Go ahead, let yourself grieve. It's okay, sweetheart."

Lissa rocked her gently as she had so many times before when the child was sick or had gotten injured playing outside. This kind of hurt would be harder to mend. Lissa wiped Lacy's face with the back of her hand.

"What happened to her boyfriend?" Lacy later asked.

"Hank? We don't know, honey. No one has seen or heard from him since."

Lacy grew silent.

"But that's how I got you. You weren't my baby, but you are still part of my flesh and blood. You understand that, right, honey? You're the best thing that came out of that tragedy." She reached across to hold Lacy's hand. "And your daddy, before he died, adored you to pieces." She smiled her best smile and kissed Lacy on her bandaged forehead. Lissa brushed the tears from her own face and continued to hold Lacy. "I love you, baby," she whispered. "And I always will."

Lissa lovingly gazed at her daughter and, once again, fondly remembered Cousin Maria. Just then, her Aunt Celia appeared in the doorway with Uncle Charlie right behind her.

"Oh, hi," Lissa said, waving them in. She got up and gave each of them a warm hug. "I'm so glad you came."

"Is she all right?" Celia asked in a hushed voice.

"Yes, yes, the doctor said she's going to be fine."

Celia moved to Lacy's bed and smothered her with kisses. "How are you, honey? You had us all so worried."

"Hi," Lacy said, her voice soft.

"When she's well enough, I want her to come visit us—both of you," Celia said to Lissa.

"Oh, Aunt Celia, that would be great. I'm sure she'd love to."

"For a long weekend...or maybe to the mountains…"

"Anywhere she can be safe," Uncle Charlie added, decidedly.

While everyone stood around her bed, another question hung in Lissa's mind. She struggled whether to bring it up in front of the others and wondered if it were better to wait until later when her daughter was feeling up to par. Though now seemed just as good a time as any.

"Lacy, honey," Lissa began, treading lightly. "I understand you wanting to run away from an uncomfortable situation, I really do. But there were other ways you could have handled this without getting into a stranger's car, right? You know how I feel about you talking to strangers, let alone getting into their cars."

"But Mom, it wasn't a stranger's car."

"So you're saying you got into a car driven by someone you knew?"

"Yes, Mom. It was my friend, Mr. McCall."

"Mr. McCall?" she repeated. The only McCall she knew was Donny McCall from school.

"What did he look like? Was he wearing a baseball cap?"

"I think so, why?"

"Donny McCall?" Lissa said, eyeing Brian questioningly. "Remember him, Brian? He went to our school and was a year younger than we were. Short little kid with the freckles?"

Brian pondered a moment while Lissa turned back to Lacy.

"I'm wondering why he would want to pick you up, Lacy?"

"He drives a taxi, Mom. He waved at me." She paused. "The ride was my idea. I asked him to take me home."

The yellow taxi.

Chapter Forty

All but a few thin strips of light pierced through the blinds and fell across the room like daggers. His head and arm were bundled in heavy bandages resembling a horror movie mummy-like figure. The other arm bore contusions the color of ripe plums. Lissa stepped softly across the room in the manner of approaching a sleeping lion with Brian and Detective Hastings behind her. Don McCall lay quietly in bed. A nurse stood at his bedside.

"How ya doing there, Mr. McCall?" she asked with one hand on her hip.

"Could use more pain killers," he replied in a husky barely-there voice.

The nurse handed him a large pill along with a cup of water. "Here, this should help."

"Is it okay to come in now?" Lissa asked the nurse, who turned and nodded quickly.

Lissa moved slowly toward his bed. "Hey, Donny. How are you doing?"

"What are—?"

"We heard what happened," Lissa said, turning to Brian. "You remember Brian Pickering from school, right?"

"Hey, Don," Brian said with a nod.

"Right now, I'm so loaded up on pain killers, I couldn't tell ya who my nurse was."

Brian grinned. "It's okay, buddy. Don't sweat it."

"How are you?" Lissa asked.

"Seen better days, but I guess I'll make it," he said, groggily.

"I'm so sorry, Donny," she said, "I…um, we—all of us—just want to thank you."

"Thank me? For what?"

"For Lacy."

Donny drew a questioning look. "Huh? I—I don't know what ya mean."

Lissa looked over at the detective who stood off to the side by the bathroom door. "This is Detective Hastings. He's been leading the search party looking for my daughter, Lacy. She's been missing for—oh, I don't know—it seemed like an eternity to me—"

The detective's phone rang.

"Then we got word she was found safe and sound. Hopefully, she'll be more sound in a few days."

"What happened to her?"

"She was in an accident. *Your* accident. In the cab."

A curious look came over him.

"My accident?" he said, attempting to process her words. "You mean, the little girl who…was your daughter?" He frowned. "Oh, hell on earth. I am so sorry. I didn't mean any harm. I just—"

"Shhhh…we know, Donny. It's okay." Lissa patted the bed sheet to assuage him. "Thank you for wanting to help her. I appreciate it with all my heart. She told us all about you."

"How is she? Is she all right?"

"Yes, not to worry, she'll be fine. Just a broken arm and some bruises."

Don's mouth curled downward. "She was so upset when she got into the cab. I asked her what she was doing walking by herself, and she kinda mumbled something. Poor kid. She asked me to take her home, and I told her sure."

"She mentioned you before," Lissa began. "Or the *friend* she told me about...someone she met when walking Toby—that's our landlady's dog." She shook her head. "I admit that I often don't pay attention to everything she says. Kids, you know how they prattle on and on sometimes. I thought you were just some other kid like her friend, Tommy, or somebody from her school."

"She was fascinated by my spotting scope. I'm out in the woods a lot...take pictures of birds and nature, that kinda thing. I can attach my camera to it to take pictures. I took her picture once." He brightened. "You know, she looks exactly like you—when you were her age. I never realized it until after I took her picture and then I remembered you and wondered...but I never got a chance to ask her."

"She does, doesn't she?" Lissa said. "Same hair and eyes, I guess."

"I'm embarrassed to say this, but I had such a crush on you," Don managed to say in an almost whisper. "Maybe that's why I was so taken with her."

Lissa smiled and briefly glanced at Brian. "I liked you, too, Donny."

"I can't believe that little girl is your daughter." He wiped his eyes with his free hand. "This is unbelievable."

Outside the room, she noticed Detective Hastings in the hallway by the nurse's station on the phone. A moment later, someone appeared at the doorway.

****

Camera in hand, Jason Stokely headed for the precinct's dark room. He organized the space himself out of the tiny restroom at the end of the hall not being used. When the plumbing finally took its toll and the toilet was no longer serviceable, he figured a darkroom made good use out of the unused space.

Jason turned off the safelight and took the film out, cut the end, and loaded it onto the reel. He followed the standard directions—stop bath, fixer—and let them fully agitate in the chemicals to ensure a thorough surface coverage before placing it in the developing tank. Afterward he washed and agitated the film before hanging it. Fifteen minutes later, he retrieved the negatives and prepped them for printing in the enlarger.

"Sergeant Matthews?" Joe called from the doorway. "The pictures are ready."

The sergeant sat at his cluttered desk with one hand on the phone and the other holding a half-eaten donut. "Good work, Stokely," he said through a mouthful. "I'll be right there."

****

Officer Dwayne McCall stepped into the hospital room. He nodded to Brian and Lissa on the approach to his brother's bedside.

"Looks like there's someone here to see you," Lissa said to Don, stepping away from the bed. "I guess we'll be leaving now." She looked up at Dwayne, who stood head and shoulders above her. "We're old school mates," she said, smiling at him.

"This is my big brother," Don told them.

"Hi, pleased to meet you," Lissa said, extending

her hand, "and this is Brian Pickering."

"Pickering? Do I know you?" Dwayne asked.

"Grew up in Pinewood."

"Yeah, but—oh, aren't you a former cop or something?"

"D.O.D," he replied modestly.

"That's right." He extended his hand to Brian. "I remember you from your presentation at one of the security conferences a couple of years back."

Lissa moved toward the doorway and noticed the detective still on the phone.

Dwayne moved toward Don's bed. "So what's goin' on, man? You feelin' any better today?"

"I guess so."

"What's the doc say?"

"He's been AWOL, so who knows for sure."

Dwayne paused before speaking. "I, um...I have some bad news," Dwayne said, taking a seat by the bed after Lissa and Brian left.

"Wha'd'ya mean?" Don shifted under the covers.

"The police..." he began."

"What about them?"

"They think that..." He shook his head. "And it's crazy, but they think you're the Peeping Tom they've been looking for."

Don's gaze turned stony. "What?" His voice rose in anger. "They think I'm a Peeping Tom? What the—how they'd get that idea?"

"Your telescope."

"It's a *spotting* scope. I use it to spot birds. I'm a birder—not a stalker."

"Tell that to the police."

"What...am I arrested?"

"They already have a warrant for your tele—I mean, spotting scope. I saw them haul it out."

"So next, they'll get a warrant for my arrest, is that it?"

"I'm sorry—"

"I'm in no condition to go to jail, Dwayne."

"I know, I know. Don't worry about it. I'm just giving you a heads-up. Look, it's one thing to get an arrest but a whole other thing to get jail time. It's categorized as disorderly conduct, a misdemeanor with a maximum sentence of a year in—"

"A year? Dwayne, I didn't do anything, not a gosh darn thing, man. I didn't enter anyone's property or stare in any windows, nothin' like that. This stinks."

"I'm doing all I can to convince them, bro, I really am."

"So how'd they track me down?"

"Dunno. I guess someone saw you going up to wherever you spot the birds—so where is that anyway?"

"In the neighborhood, over by the swim club near Apple Valley road. There's a walking trail in there and the woods go back pretty deep."

"That's near a residential area. I guess someone spotted you and thought the worst."

Chapter Forty-One

Officer Matthews unclipped the pictures Jason Stokely hung in the dark room. Each one a black and white photograph. His brow furrowed. One-by-one, he sorted through them while shaking his head back and forth.

"These are...what are they? They're all like something out of a wild life magazine. Looks like a bunch of trees and birds here...you develop the whole roll, Stokely?"

"Yes, sir, it's a 24-shot roll, and only twenty-one shots that are good. That's all, sir."

"This is it?" Officer Matthews's mouth hung open. "This all you got? If this guy's a Peeping Tom, he's got a fetish for birds. That's about it. You sure this is the right roll of film?"

"Yes, sir. I'm positive. I took it out of the camera myself."

He went through the photos a second time and then got up. "Thanks, Stokely. Good work, but I guess we're back to square one."

Jason collected the pictures. "Do you want me to keep them anyway?"

Officer Matthews shrugged, "Yeah, might as well date and file them."

"Okay, will do, sir. Looks like there's already a date on them. Says July 18."

"Good enough."

Jason counted the pictures again and then brought them down the hall to Dorinda Walcott.

"Hi, Dorinda, can you file these? They're the photo evidence from the camera...the guy they think is the Peeping Tom."

"Oh, sure. The Don McCall case. I've got the file started already."

When he handed the pile of photos to her, something caught his attention. "Wait, can I see them again, please?" Jason stared at the photo on the top of the pile. "Do you have a magnifying glass?"

"I used to have one somewhere," she said, rummaging through her desk. "Yep, here it is."

He took the picture and held it up against the window and brought the magnifying glass in close. "Hmmm, this is interesting."

"What is it?" she asked.

"I don't know, but I think Sarge ought to have a look."

****

"So—" Sergeant Matthews began, staring at the picture. "What am I looking at here? Looks like a bird, Stokely." The photograph depicted a black-capped bird with a long tail sitting on top of a branch.

"Look in the background, sir."

In the upper right corner of the photo, a semi-blurred figure appeared on the stairway adjacent to a clapboard house.

"Ah, okay. Looks like a female...dark hair." The sergeant looked up at him. "So?"

"I don't know, sir, but I just thought it might be something," said Jason. "Just a gut feeling."

213

Sergeant Matthews focused on the picture.

"And this other one," Jason said, "has the same girl looking inside the window. It's not unusual until you see her doing this." He handed him a third picture that showed the same girl bending down in front of the door and inserting something long into the doorknob.

"Something about this looks familiar." Officer Matthews turned over the picture. "It's dated July 18." He checked the incident report log for the eighteenth of July and noted a break-in reported on Bellevue Avenue at just after seven p.m.

Chapter Forty-Two

"Thanks, Dr. Billing. Yes, she's coming home today," Lissa bubbled to her boss on the phone. "I'm on my way to pick her up now. My friend, Brian, is taking me. We're almost at the hospital. Yes, sir. Thank you for your understanding. Will do." She snapped her phone shut. "My boss is so great, so accommodating. Best boss I've ever had." She leaned in to give him a kiss.

"What's that for?" Brian asked at the wheel.

"For everything. If not for you, I don't know what I would have done."

"What have I done?" He grinned shyly.

"Oh, stop with your modesty." She slapped his arm. "You were only my rock, that's all. Hey, by the way, I'm feeling hungry."

"Did you eat this morning?"

"Actually, I forgot to—"

"To eat?"

"To pick up groceries."

"It'll be a while before we get there. Do you want to stop somewhere first?"

"No, let's wait 'til we get to the hospital. The dining room there is always open."

"Okay, but we can always stop at a Quik Mart or someplace to pick up something for the ride. Besides, I need gas. The tank is near empty."

"Okay, then. As long as you're stopping anyway, I could really go for a cream cheese bagel right about now."

A few miles up the road, a sign for food and fuel indicated a rest stop. Brian pulled in and got out to fuel up. "So you want a poppy bagel with cream cheese or plain?"

"Plain is fine."

"Want coffee, too?"

"Sure, that'll be great," she said with a nod. "A couple of creamers, too, and plenty of napkins."

When Brian left, Lissa turned on the radio. WBAL's news reporter, Art Aikens, updated information about the seven-car pile-up and subsequent closure of I-340. Next, Aikens introduced a local break-in story that included a voiceover of an interview with Pinewood's Chief of Police. She turned up the volume and listened.

"Brian," she said excitedly as soon as he came back. "The radio report—it just mentioned the break-in. *My* break-in." She pointed to the radio.

"What? What did it say?" he asked, handing her the bag.

"The police chief said they had a lead on it, something about recent vandalism in the neighborhood, and they also tied it in with my break-in."

"Did they mention any names?"

"No, but they have a suspect."

****

Entering Lacy's hospital room, Lissa could see her daughter's improvement. Clear-eyed and smiling. With the exception of the broken arm, her daughter was back to her cheery, normal self. Hopefully, the emotional backwash would heal just as quickly. Only time would tell. Lissa prayed God would spare her daughter any serious repercussions. Lissa's joy overwhelmed her, and she wanted to kiss everyone in the hospital.

On the ride home, Lissa noticed Brian was unusually quiet ever since he took the phone call in the hallway of the hospital.

"Everything all right, Bri?" she asked once they got onto the main roadway.

He shook his head.

"What is it?"

"Angela called."

A stab of anxiety hit her chest and wound its way into her loins, cinching her stomach. She always wondered about his wife possibly getting back together with him and worried that one day it would happen. "What…" she began hesitantly, "what did she say?" The weight of the words gave her pause. While she was curious, she was equally frightened of what he might say.

He shook his head again. "It's Madison."

"Madison? What about her?"

"It's not good. She's in juvenile hall."

Chapter Forty-Three

"I'll be right back," Lissa called to Lacy, who sat on the living room sofa in front of the TV engrossed in a cartoon. "I'm just going downstairs to drop off the rent check."

Lacy barely moved a muscle, wrapped cocoon-like in the afghan her great-grandmother made. The jade green wool softened over the years along with the unraveling of some of the stitches, but the comfort of the yarn trumped its looks. She held a cup of hot cocoa on her lap and beside her, a bag of mini marshmallows.

"Go easy on those marshmallows, please," Lissa called before opening the door.

"I know, Mom," she replied, still focused on the TV.

When Lissa stepped outside, she noticed Mrs. Houser's son, Drew, take a leap off the last step and dart around the side of the house. In the corner of the landing by the railing sat a small poinsettia plant. She glanced back down the stairs and wondered if little Drew recently placed it there. A smile crept onto her face.

Lissa heard the sound of voices around the side of the house and spotted Mrs. Houser. With a wave, she called down to her, "Good morning." Mrs. Houser waved back.

"His body suffers from palsy, but his mind is

intact," she said later to Lissa. "He has such a lovely spirit, though." She smiled. "Actually, I think my Drew has a crush on your little girl."

"Oh, that's so sweet. Really?" Lissa asked, taken aback at the revelation.

"Yes, in fact, I saw him one morning with a pair of my pinking shears outside by the rose bushes. You know, Miss Rucker has the loveliest grandifloras out back. Have you seen them?"

Lissa nodded. "Oh, yes, I love her roses. They're gorgeous."

"Yes, well, I saw Drew cutting a rose from one of her bushes. It was probably the last of the blooms for the year. I hope Miss Rucker didn't see." She shook her head with disapproval. "It was very early in the morning when he usually goes out to walk Miss Rucker's dog. When he came back, I asked him why he took my sheers and he sheepishly confessed about cutting a rose for his 'girl.' I laughed to myself because he doesn't have a girlfriend," she said with a shrug, "but I figured it was little Lacy."

"You know, we wondered who left the rose. It's funny, I always thought it was for *me*." She covered her mouth and dipped her head in mock embarrassment.

Lissa picked up the plant and brought it into the house.

"Look what someone left for you, Lace." Lissa placed the poinsettia on the coffee table in front of her.

"For me?" she questioned, curiously.

"You have a secret admirer."

"Who?" she asked, unfazed.

"Drew."

"Next door Drew?"

"Uh huh." Lissa nodded happily.

"Why?"

"Probably a get-well gift."

"Okay," she said and went back to watching the TV.

****

"Hi, Robin, it's me," Lissa said flatly.

"Hey, girl. What's wrong? You sound depressed."

"My whole life's falling apart," she said. Lissa looked out the window into the gray winter sky. *This is what happens when you get in over your head.* She pulled the shade down and sank onto the couch.

"What happened? Dear Lord, don't tell me they found something wrong with Lacy."

"No, no, she's doing great, thank God. Improving daily. She's back in school. Everything is coming along fine with her. Her cast will come off in another week, the doctor said." She paused and lowered her voice. "It's Brian."

"Oh?"

"It looks like we're breaking up. Or already did."

"Oh, that stinks. Sorry to hear that, sweetie. Why? What happened?"

Lissa sighed. "There's so much going on with his life right now—his marriage, or what's left of it...and now his daughter. The oldest one. She's in trouble."

"What kind?"

"Remember the break-in at the apartment back in the summer? Turns out his daughter, of all people, is involved."

"His *daughter?*"

"Yep."

"How old is she?"

"Seventeen or maybe eighteen by now."

"That's crazy. Why would she do that?"

"I have no idea. I can't even get my head wrapped around it." She sighed again and started gnawing her lower lip. "But ever since then, Brian's been emotionally MIA. It's been six days since we last spoke." She bit her lip and silently cursed herself for getting involved with a married man.

"Aw, I had such hopes for you guys."

"When I called him on it, he sounded a bit evasive. But the take-home message I got was that he thinks we should cool things off."

"Do you think he's getting back with his wife?"

"I don't think so," she replied, and continued speaking as evenly as she could, despite her fractured heart. "He told me a while back she's asked for a divorce, and he seemed pretty intent on following through with it. She probably has a boyfriend. I don't think there's anything between them—not that he hadn't tried to keep things together at one point. I think he made peace with the idea a long time ago. But why he's leaving me out in the cold is the weird part."

"I'm so sorry, Liss. I wish there was something I could do to help you," she said sweetly.

"Your prayers would be helpful."

"I'll always pray for you, my friend. You know that."

"Thanks. I need prayer now more than ever. Every time I turn around, there's something else."

"It's always something, right?"

"This side of heaven…" Lissa's words trailed off.

"We can worry ourselves to death about things or we can turn over our cares to the Lord. I always ask myself, which is easier?"

"Sometimes, I'll have to admit, I like licking my wounds."

"Tell me about it," Robin drawled.

"Oh," Lissa said, "by the way, the mystery of the pink rose is solved."

"Pink rose? Oh, right. Who sent it?"

"Actually, it was hand-delivered by a neighbor boy."

"A boy?"

"Yep. Name's Drew. Sweet little kid about Lacy's age. He has some kind of palsy, but it's not cerebral."

"Does he have a crush on you or something?"

"Not *me*—Lacy."

"How cute."

"It is. Oh, and he also left her a poinsettia plant. It's strange, but he has the best timing."

"The best timing…how so?"

"It's just that every time something goes screwy— he seems to have some kind of extra-sensory perception. The rose, after the break-in, and now after her injury, a poinsettia plant. He's shown more compassion than some adults I know."

"That's so sweet. Hey, what are you doing for Christmas?"

Lissa blew a breath into the phone. "It's hard for me to get into the mood this year…I don't know. Ever since the incident…" Her voice trailed. "We've been invited to my aunt and uncle's, and if we don't go, it'll be even harder to explain why."

"Just go. Try to enjoy yourself, and don't worry about Brian. Leave it all on the altar, right?"

A lopsided manger scene with only two wise men

and one tiny sheep standing in front of baby Jesus sat on the credenza. She had no idea what happened to the third wise man statue that carried the myrrh. Apparently, gold and frankincense were all the gifts the baby was receiving this year. It seemed everyone was getting something but her. With reminders of Christmas everywhere, Lissa wished the New Year were already here.

"I thought he was serious about me. Now I feel so stupid."

"I'm so sorry, Liss. Give it time. If things are meant to be, they'll be. You know that. Just give it some time."

"Thanks, Robin, you're right."

What choice do I have?

Her thoughts turned to Lacy. She had her daughter back; her prayers were answered. *Hallelujah.* But after recovering from the crisis of almost losing Lacy, the loss of Brian crushed her fragile emotions all over again. Her heavy heart, delicate as glass, shattered once more.

Chapter Forty-Four

January 2, 2006

The doorbell rang and Lissa's heart leaped. Brian weighed on her mind so much that every time her phone rang or the doorbell buzzed, she hoped it was him. She played the scenario in her mind over and over again thinking the separation between them was a bad dream. They had so much in common and were friends for so long; to throw their relationship away now just didn't make sense.

Lissa glanced in the mirror. Pale face and greasy hair stared back at her. This time she hoped it wasn't Brian. Of all the times for him to come back. She thought twice about answering. When her curiosity took over as to who was there, she moved to the door and peeked through the peephole. A woman and someone else stood beside her. *Someone selling something?*

She opened the door and soon recognized the woman, having met her at one of the school's PTA meetings. A friendly sort, they bonded quickly with each other.

"Judy?"

"Hi, Lissa," the woman said soberly. She bore a sad, disappointed smile. "I hope we're not disturbing you or anything."

"No, not a bit," she said, pulling the door open.

Judy entered, head down, as though marching to her death, followed by a young girl whom she judged as only slightly older than Lacy. Her full, angelic lips were carved into a stoic mannequin-like face. Lissa couldn't get a read on her. Shy? Embarrassed? With her stiff body language, it was obvious the child was uncomfortable and resistant to being in the room.

"So what brings you here?" she asked. "I assume this is your daughter?"

"Yes, this is my daughter, Simone," the woman said flatly, glancing at her child, who refused to make eye contact and fixed her gaze on the floor. "I wouldn't normally barge in on someone like this, but I thought it important."

"Oh, it's fine," Lissa swatted her hand to make light of it. "Hello, Simone," Lissa said. "Pleased to meet you. Why don't you both have a seat." Lissa gestured toward the sofa.

"Actually, Lissa, I'd rather we stood." She glanced over at Simone. "My daughter has something she wants to say to you." She focused on the girl and with her eyes, prompted her to speak.

Silence rose like a roar in the room. After a while, the girl looked up at her mother and again toward the floor before she began to speak. "I—um," she began and let her eyes roam everywhere but toward Lissa. "My mother says that—I mean, I wanted to say that I'm sorry…sorry for what I said to Lacy."

"To Lacy?" Lissa searched Simone for a clue. "I'm afraid I don't understand, honey. What did you say that you're sorry for?"

The child looked down again.

"Lissa, I'm afraid it was my daughter who caused

the trouble at Becca Robson's party."

"Oh?" *The mystery unravels.*

"I'm so embarrassed to say but Simone confessed that it was she who told Lacy she was adopted."

The words hit like a thunderbolt. The infernal night came back with all its renditions. The grief and anxiety. The pain that slammed into her like a train at full speed. The breath knocked so far out of her she couldn't breathe. A night she never wanted to relive. She took a step back mentally and attempted to parse her words in a measured tone that gave nothing away as to her disdain for this impish child.

"Oh," Lissa nodded slowly, "so that's how it—" she said, clipping her sentence. The words hung in the air. Her emotions tugged in all directions. She folded her arms across her chest. She wanted to slap the girl silly but then thought better of it. *Okay, be nice. She's just a child. A brat but still someone's child. What would Jesus do right now?* The question floated in her mind like a neon sign. Lately, every move she made seemed to be processed by asking the same noble question. Of course, Jesus would turn the other cheek. That's what he'd do.

The moments passed, and Lissa looked from Judy to Simone and back again. A fragile battle of hidden anguish harbored between them. The desire to raise a hand to the child dissolved, and she put herself in the girl's shoes. Not that she was happy but for the sake of the girl, the progress being attempted counted for something. Judy's close-set eyes riveted on Lissa, who saw in them a mix of sympathy and regret. Lissa sensed the woman's pain.

"Lissa, I never mentioned anything to Simone, but

she must have overheard me say it—somehow—to my husband is the only way I can imagine." Her gaze leveled with Lissa's. "After you told me about the adoption—you know, at the PTA, we were talking about it—my husband and me. We'd read the story in the paper about the anniversary of the big drug bust...and I remember your dad was famous for putting away Joe Hellinger. It so happens my husband is related to the Hellingers. Thankfully, by marriage only." She rolled her eyes. "So we were talking about you and Lacy and, well, I'm so terribly—"

"No, no, Judy, please," Lissa interjected. "Don't fret over it. What's done is done." Lissa understood her embarrassment. She placed her hand on the woman's arm to underscore her sincerity. "It's in the past now. It's fine. Lacy's been officially told now, by me, of course. And she understands. Really, she's okay now." *Just okay, not great. Maybe one day.* Lissa tried to put a happy face on it but deep down knew it would be awhile before her daughter was truly great.

Then Judy moved toward Lissa and ushered her into the kitchen. Her eyebrows knit as she whispered, "She's a bit brazen, I'm afraid. I don't understand where the mean streak comes from but believe me, my husband and I are dealing with it as best we can."

Lissa nodded sympathetically.

"My husband puts so much pressure on her to— well, be the best. I'm sure that must have something to do with it. We're looking into counseling..." Her soft voice trailed off.

"Judy, I understand. Kids will be kids, right?" Lissa lent a small, knowing look. "We can't control them every minute."

Judy hung her head apologetically. Lissa saw the toll on the woman's face. Her hands shook, and she looked a bit older than the last time they met at school. When they first met, Lissa saw her as someone most likely her age or younger. Now, the woman seemed to have gained ground on her.

Lissa sympathized with Judy's predicament, realizing, like Judy, she wanted to control her own daughter's comings and goings just as much as any other mother. Her own words echoed in her head... *we can't control them every minute.* How well she knew. The timely dance between nurture and suffocation was a balance that would always weigh challenging, but for now, Lissa was relieved that the hardest battle she would probably ever face was over. She was grateful she and Lacy were able to move past the wall that separated them since the child's birth. Now that Lacy knew about her birth mother, there would be no more secrets between them.

The two women went back to the living area where Simone lingered alone by the fireplace, running her finger along one of the stones. Lissa glanced at Lacy's bedroom door in the shadows of the hallway. The warbling of Britney Spears seeped through the walls.

Lissa thanked them for coming, even praising Simone for being "a big girl" in admitting her wrong doing. "Maybe there's a lesson in this," Lissa said to Judy as she opened the front door for them. "For all of us."

Outside, the afternoon air was crisp yet still and the sunlight bounced sharply off the newly fallen snow. She closed the door. Bright light poured into the southwest-facing window, melting the frost that clung for most of the morning. Lissa moved toward the light and traced a smiley face on the glass.

Chapter Forty-Five

Two months later

"So what do you think, Lacy—of Florida?" Lissa asked while at the computer.

"Florida?" She glanced up from the floor where she sat drawing at the coffee table. Her eyes brightened. "For vacation?"

"Maybe," she replied, clicking through pictures of Florida. She paused at a photo of a flock of seagulls at sea where the photographer exquisitely captured the bird's flight juxtaposed with the red-orange glow of a persimmon sun flirting at the horizon. She imagined the sounds of their awkward high-pitched squawks as they floated in the air. How enviable, their freedom. What would make the picture even more perfect would be sharing the white beach in the foreground with Brian. She wanted to be there with him, laying in the warm sand while he rubbed her body in coconut-scented sun block cream as warm breezes from the ocean caressed them under the setting sun.

Lissa knew how much Lacy loved Florida from the time she begged to go down south to see her old school mate after the girl's family moved to St. Petersburg late last summer. Back in Bryn Mawr, the children in Lacy's class often came home from Christmas or Easter break beaming with tanned skin from their sunny vacations. Something Lissa could never afford to give her daughter. With some of her accrued insurance money, she thought a trip—anywhere—would be in order. For her, to clear her head, and for Lacy, an opportunity to get some tropical color in her cheeks.

Lissa scrolled through pages of information on Florida, in particular, West Palm Beach where some distant cousins lived. Wading through pictures of cool blue water, pink and white homes donning Spanish-style rooftops, and bright sun and surf, the idea of vacationing in Florida didn't seem as elusive to her as she once thought. A bug or two, along with hot temperatures, now paled in comparison to the gorgeous pictures evoking the luxury of balmy Florida.

Lacy slipped onto her lap at the computer while she clicked through the virtual online brochures of rental properties overlooking the ocean. One displayed a paver patio and river rocks like a page out of *Architectural Digest*. "Looks pretty, doesn't it?" Lissa asked and handed the mouse to Lacy to take control for a while. "Must cost a fortune to rent that. Keep clicking, Lace."

"I want to stay at Emma's house," Lacy said.

"Well, I'm not sure, Lace. We haven't really received an actual invitation, you know, formally." Lissa tried to recall what Emma's mother wrote in the Christmas card she sent to them.

"Oh," she said, and slid back to the floor where she picked up a colored pencil and began drawing. Lissa stared at Lacy's artwork on the coffee table.

"Who's in your picture, honey?"

She half-shrugged. "Just some people."

With a yellow crayon, she drew hair on top of a tall

figure's head. The outline resembled none other than Brian. She tried so many times to rid images of him from her head, yet some of the pictures Lacy drew only reinforced him. In one, Lacy drew a tall man along with two short women inside the outline of a house with a smoking chimney. She wondered if Lacy missed him, too.

Her thoughts drew to the last few days they spent together. She rehashed the video in her head, allowing snippets of the reel to play out over and over. She couldn't stop thinking about him and felt caught in the trap of her mind. *Where was he? Why was he so distant? What did I do to deserve this cold treatment?*

Chapter Forty-Six

Thoughts of Brian weighed heavily on her heart; so many times she wanted to call him, hoping for the opportunity to buttonhole him on what went wrong.

What happened between us, Bri? What did I do? Please tell me. He owed her that much. She went through the motions of their imagined conversation, practicing what she would say in the privacy of her room, hoping to turn her thoughts into a reality of sorts or something to assuage her desperate curiosity. Though, every time she felt compelled to reach out, something pulled her back. Pride? The Lord? She couldn't tell.

If the Lord didn't want them together, she certainly didn't either. What's the sense of cajoling or twisting another's will for the sake of a relationship? She saw enough of that with her own family, particularly in the sad affairs of her cousin, Maria.

She reached for the phone and mentally rehearsed what she wanted to say before pressing the automatic dial button. In the second before the call connected, she quickly hung up. Would he think it a desperate ploy to get back together? In her heart, she knew otherwise. She pressed the automatic dial button again. In the moments before he picked up, her pulse quickened. Though nervous, she hung on, committed to following through on her decision to connect with him. When he began to speak, she quickly realized she reached his recorded voicemail message. Short and to the point, *"Hi, it's Brian, you know the drill."* Her mind froze. She couldn't compose her thoughts and quickly hung up.

She went to the kitchen and made a cup of tea and then settled down to do her weekly report for Dr. Billing. Working from home proved to be a blessing. After a couple of hours, she took a break and went for a walk. She opened the door and startled at the figure standing before her at the threshold. For a moment, she couldn't speak.

Brian stood at the doorstep resembling a J. Crew model in a white oxford shirt and faded jeans. "Hey, Liss." His voice quivered, lacking its usual confidence, and sounded as though it would fracture at any moment. "How'r you?" His eyes met hers and the electricity between them buzzed. *Better now,* she thought. In Pinewood, the expression, *better than I deserve,* was commonplace. She felt all of the above. Elated to see him, her heart thrummed, and she wondered why he'd come. Not setting herself up for disappointment was a no-brainer. She was no longer a teenager ready to give her heart away. No, not this time.

"Brian, what are you doing here?" she asked levelly. The air thickened between them.

"I came to give these to you," he replied, and pulled around a large bouquet of roses—in pink, yellow, and red with a spray of baby's breath—from behind him.

Her heart melted. *A bit old-fashioned but still sweet.*

"Can we talk?" he asked, sheepishly.

Without a word, she parted the door wider to invite him to enter and took the flowers to the kitchen sink. She soaked them in cool water until she could find a suitable vase; the flower arranging could wait. Lissa came out from the kitchen and curled up in the chair across from the fireplace where he stood, his expression forlorn. *Did he want to resume their old course? Establish a friendship? Or was his news something more serious?*

"Lissa, my wife passed away." His words came out soft, but the impact sent a shockwave to her core.

"Passed away?" She paused to collect her thoughts. She *died?* "Oh, that's awful. From what?"

"She had ovarian cancer, stage III a while back. We thought it was in remission. She was but then—" He shook his head.

"Oh, I'm so sorry, Bri…" *A fleeting thought that he'd come to tell her he was moving away came to mind. He's lost his wife and now she was losing him— forever.*

A chasm of silence rose in the room.

"That's why I couldn't continue our relationship," he continued. "I felt so guilty. Even though I knew my wife didn't love me anymore, or like she once did, while she lay dying, I had to do my part as a husband— separated or not." His eyes misted, and she could barely contain her emotions. "My feelings for you never went away, Liss. In fact, during our own remission, of sorts, I think my feelings for you increased." He held her gaze. "I'm so sorry…sorry that I was distant." She tried to hold back from crying along with him as he wiped his eyes with the back of his sleeve. "It wasn't you, Lissa. It wasn't anything you did or said…please understand that." His face—a portrait of grief—folded as he held back his emotions. "I was so distraught…over what Madison did. It was too embarrassing." He hung his head. She rose from the chair and walked toward the window.

"But why…why would she do that? Break into my apartment?"

"Madison knew there was trouble between Angie and me, and she said she wanted to see who the new woman in my life was."

"Seriously? But how did she know where I lived?"

A line drew to his lips. "She followed you, Liss."

"Followed me?" *What is this, a soap opera?*

He nodded. "She borrowed Angie's car. That's what she said…she admitted it in so many words, that is." He paused. "Angie drove a white SUV."

Lissa stared at him in disbelief. *The white SUV.* A chill crept up her leg. "So you're saying all this…the stalking, breaking open the lock…it was all because she was upset and…and curious…about *me*?"

"Appears so. That's her alibi, anyway."

"Sounds like she was just trying to make trouble." She folded her arms across her chest.

He abruptly stood. "And she did. Big time. Not only for herself but for—well, for everyone."

"I'll have to agree with you there."

"I even caught her at my computer—she made an excuse, but she turned three shades of red while explaining what she was doing."

Lissa moved toward the front window and she looked out into the early evening sky. Their first date came into focus, the day they met at the restaurant by the train station, and the overwhelming feeling of being watched by the tracks while waiting for him to show up.

She turned to him. "What was she doing on your computer?"

He lowered his eyes and shook his head.

Possible scenarios circled in Lissa's mind, including the fact that Madison may have snooped into her father's FB account and read his personal messages. If so, she knew exactly when and where her dad would be that day. And who he'd be with. *Clever girl.*

She let her feelings about it settle. Brian had enough going on right now without her throwing the misdeeds of his daughter into the mix. What did it matter how she'd come to know about their relationship? She did and that was that.

"But, you know what?" Lissa began. "I feel more upset for her than for me. If I look at it from her perspective, she must have really been disturbed..." Lissa's voice trailed off.

Brian moved into her space. She wanted to push him away but something stirred within her. She fought her feelings to keep him at bay, frightened at what was happening right now.

"Lissa—I," Brian's voice faltered. "I want you to know that I never stopped thinking about you or—wanting you." His mournful eyes drew her in.

His words stunned and she braced herself, not knowing whether to give in or keep her guard up. Once bitten, twice shy. Though, for her, it was *twice* bitten. Secretly, she put her heart out there for him more than once. Maybe if she'd let him in on her feelings back in school, things would be different. The idea of having her heart slammed chafed her sensibilities. She assured herself it wouldn't happen again.

"I never wanted to hurt you or—" He glanced away.

When he looked back, his eyes shone glassy. "I love you, Lissa."

The peaceful calm of a deep river unleashed inside, releasing her anxiety.

"Brian—I don't know what to say." A floating sensation came over her as he reached for her hands and pulled her forward.

"Don't say anything, Lissa. Just give me a sign that you feel the same way."

With that, he took her in his arms and kissed her like she'd never been kissed before.

Chapter Forty-Seven

"Hannah and Lacy really get along well," Lissa said as she looked out the window into the back yard where the girls were tossing a Frisbee with Drew. "We are so blessed, Bri."

Brian came up behind her and put his arms around her waist and she leaned into him.

"So where do you want to go for lunch?" he asked.

"Oh, I don't know. Have any suggestions?" she cooed.

"I want you for lunch," he said, nuzzling her neck. Lissa playfully slapped his face. "Seriously."

"I am serious." He kissed her deeply and then pulled away. "What?"

"We haven't been to The Train Stop in a while," she said.

He sighed. "Ah, the little caboose. I thought you didn't like the noise level in there."

"I don't, but that's the first place we went before we—well, all this," she said before they locked lips for another long, lingering kiss.

"I guess the Train Stop it is," he said. "Although I'm not sure I can wait that long."

"Brian Pickering, you let me go." Lissa mock whined and squirmed her way out of his arms.

"Or how about a ride to Baltimore?" he asked. "We could go to the harbor for lunch?"

"Oh, I don't know, it's kind of late to be heading all the way to the harbor. Let's ask the girls. I know Lacy's been asking about Sugarloaf Village," Lissa said brightly. "Oh, wait. There is one place I definitely want to show you."

"Okay, you ready?" he asked.

"Yep, let's go."

****

Lissa and Brian's former elementary school sat forlorn in the afternoon light.

"It's closed," Lissa explained to him with a mock frown. "Lacy and I were here not too long ago."

"Wouldn't be the first school to shut down," Brian offered. "Sometimes, it's just a temporary thing. It could open up again later, you never know."

A wistful feeling came over her. "I wonder if it's locked."

"Probably is."

A nostalgic feeling tugged within, and she had an overwhelming desire to go inside. Turning to Brian, she said, "Mind if I get out? I want to get a closer look. I've wanted to ever since we moved back to Pinewood. It's silly, but it won't take but a minute." She held up her index finger to punctuate her words.

"Can I come, Mom?"

"No, Lacy, you stay in the car with Brian and Hannah. I'll be right back."

Standing at the top of the steps, Lissa paused. The door's dark green paint appeared chipped and faded in spots, begging for a fresh coat. She reached for the knob. The tarnished brass felt smooth in her palm. *Unlocked.* She hadn't expected an abandoned school to have an unlocked door. With a strong sense of curiosity in gear, she turned the knob and entered.

Upon stepping inside, the familiar scent of dusty cinderblock lingered in the hushed interior, same as it had over two decades ago. Goose bumps ran up her arms. *I can't believe I'm standing here.*

To the left stood the stairwell tucked within the narrow entryway. She took the stairs to the second floor and walked down the dimly lit hall. The last time she stood here, Miss Keogan was busily engaged with her students, hugging and waving goodbye for the summer. Knowing she wouldn't be coming back again in the fall because of her mother's decision to move to Pennsylvania, Lissa approached the young woman and thanked her for being such a *wonderful* teacher. Miss Keogan smiled and replied how fortunate she was to have such a lovely class, "*and especially a student like you, Lissa.*" Lissa blushed at her teacher's remark and, later, embarrassed by her own words, thought it corny for a kid to call a teacher *wonderful.*

Lissa glimpsed inside the classroom. Everything looked tiny. The windows, the blackboard. Modern metal one-piece desks in neutral beige with attached chairs replaced the old wooden ones, and the American flag no longer hung in the corner. She pictured her classmates in their seats; the most memorable being Bobby Prince, Robbie Oleberg, Patti Cotter, and Brian, who sat in the back row.

Down the hall, she observed the rest of the classrooms on the opposite side of the hallway. The open blinds in the back-to-back rooms revealed a view of the schoolyard. The blacktop sat adjacent to an overgrown grassy hill bearing a copse of shade trees along with a row of dense brush. She recalled the day when one of her classmates claimed to have witnessed a man lingering by the trees wearing a raincoat. Frightened, the girl ran back inside.

Another image rose of the time one of her classmates dared her to look inside the boy's room. Through the girl's coaxing, Lissa almost came close to following through with the brazen act of stealing a glance inside the male domain, though at the last minute, she didn't. Now, the boys' room bore the modern logo of a male figure on the front. Never seeing the inside, she reached for the handle and as she opened it, quickly realized she had absolutely no desire to look at all. She released the handle. The action met with a harsh squeal akin to a strangled cat, and the eerie sound reverberated throughout the cavernous hallway. Startled, she ran back down the hall, took the stairs two at a time, and barreled through the double doors. The sunlight and sweet spring air brought a sense of calm as she flew down the narrow steps to the car.

"See anything interesting?" Brian asked when she plopped down on the seat.

"No, nothing, really," she said, breathless. "Just nostalgia."

"Must have been some strange nostalgia. You look like you just saw a ghost or something."

"Just my imagination."

"Seen enough?" he asked, resting his hand on her knee.

"Yep, I'm good, thanks."

As he pulled slowly around the circular driveway, he asked, "So why did you want to come back to see the old school?"

Lissa paused. "It's…well, it's kinda weird, really. But it's where we met." She glanced back at the school. "And there was a picture on Facebook that kind of hit a sweet spot with me about school days. Remember May Day Fun Night…fourth grade?"

"Vaguely."

She leaned back. "I couldn't get your attention for anything."

A puzzled look came over him. "What are you talking about?"

Lissa blushed, embarrassed at bringing it up.

"We were pretty tight as I recall," he said.

"No, no, I mean like a *girlfriend*," she said coyly.

"We were only, what, ten years old?"

She grinned. "You liked Patti Cotter that way…I could tell."

"Patti Cotter?" He blew out a puff of air. "I think you've got the wrong guy."

"How so?"

"Patti Cotter liked Bobby Packard."

"Bobby Packard?"

"She was only using me to get to him." He relaxed his head on the back of the seat and turned his eyes toward her.

Lissa couldn't believe what she was hearing. "You mean…" she said, shaking her head, "after all these years…I had the story wrong?"

"Guess so," he replied with a smug grin.

"Now that's funny," she said, amazed at the revelation.

She gazed back at the school as they drove off and wondered how Patti and Bobby were doing. "Anyway," she began, shifting her gaze to him, "I just wanted to be here…with you—I don't know. Silly, right?" She shrugged. "Just something I needed to do. Besides, I thought you might want to see your old neighborhood. You used to live not far from here, remember?"

"Yes, I did."

"I even remember your house. We had enough play dates. Remember your club?"

"You had play dates with Brian, Mom?" Lacy leaned forward.

"Yes, honey, we did."

Brian grinned. "Your mother was the fastest runner in the whole fourth grade, Lacy."

"Cool," she replied, as he drove them down the residential street through the tree-lined neighborhood to his old house.

Chapter Forty-Eight

At The Train Stop, Brian, Lissa and the girls dined *al fresco* on veggie burgers and sweet potato fries on the upstairs patio tucked under a canopy of trees.

"Not bad," Lissa said of her burger. "You like yours?" she asked the children.

Lacy and Hannah, mouths full, nodded.

She turned to Brian. "So what's next on the agenda for today?"

He put down his coffee. "Oh, I don't know," he said with a shrug. "It's up to you. I'm outnumbered."

Lissa nodded. "True, you are."

Brian pulled out his credit card and turned to signal the waiter.

"Okay, girls, we have the power here according to Chief Pickering." She nudged him with her elbow. "What do you think might be a fun thing to do this afternoon?"

The children tossed ideas back and forth, and when the waiter approached, they giggled. Lissa teared up at seeing the rose and little black box on the tray he placed on the table.

"I have an idea," Brian began. "How about somebody proposes?"

Lissa froze. The reality of the moment practically knocked her over. She blushed, stammered, and began to tear up.

"Lissa, you mean the world to me." He reached for the ring and held it in front of her. "Will you marry me?"

Through her tears, she nodded yes, and he slipped the diamond onto her hand and kissed her squarely on the lips. The waiter and the rest of the wait staff cheered and clapped along with the girls.

"We knew, Mom. Brian told us to keep the surprise a secret."

"He did? You kept the secret so well. How long did you know?"

"When you went to the ladies' room, he told us."

"That long?" she said with a grin. "I'm sure it was hard to keep it to yourselves for all of three minutes."

Brian leaned in close to whisper, "I wanted to ask their permission, to make sure they were okay with it."

"That was sweet," Lissa said, wiping a tear away. She stared at her hand, unable to pull her gaze away from the generous diamond. "I think they approve." Lissa felt so blessed in the moment. Lacy and Hannah's ease with each other gave her joy in knowing they would soon be sisters. How fortunate for Lacy to be gaining a father and Hannah, a new mother. She hoped Brian's eldest daughter Madison would welcome the union as much as the younger girls.

"So you want to marry me?" she asked, with a giggle.

"Oh, I don't know." He gave her a mockingly curious look. "Maybe."

She slapped his arm. "Well, if you're not sure—"

"I'm *very* sure." He pulled her close.

"So when do you want to get this party started?"

"Whenever you want. I've only known you since

second grade, so I think our engagement period has practically expired by now."

"I have an idea," she said. "But I'll tell you later."

On the way out of the restaurant, as they walked back to the car, Lissa grabbed Brian's hand and said, "Hey, I wonder how Donny is? Last I heard, he was cleared from the trespassing charges and out of the hospital. Maybe he's back to work."

Around the corner on the way back to the car, Lissa craned her neck to catch a glimpse of the bus depot. Two cabs idled. "Be right back," she said hastily.

"Where you going, Mom?" Lacy called out.

"Hold on, I just want to see something," she shouted back.

"Your mom is so pretty," Hannah said to Lacy.

"*That* she is, honey," Brian said and wrapped his arms around both girl's shoulders.

As Lissa approached the cabs, she peeked inside the first one where an older man with a graying beard sat smoking a cigarette. Directly behind, another cab sat idle. She turned around to go back to the others when Donny McCall came around the corner.

"Hey, Donny," Lissa called, smiling. "So glad to see you."

"Likewise," he said, eyeing her with the same soft expression he had as a little boy when he asked her to dance.

"How are you doing since the accident?"

"Better," he said with an exaggerated nod. "Much better." He pulled his hand around and pointed to the exact vertebrae. "I still have some numbness in my lower back...right here. But all things considered, I'm doin' good." He paused and shuffled his feet. A shadow fell over his eyes. "How's your daughter?"

Lissa smiled. "Oh, she's great, absolutely fine. She's done a complete turnaround." She emphasized the word *complete,* hoping to assuage any lingering guilt he may have harbored over the road accident.

He brightened. "Glad to hear it, really glad."

She nodded, and then remembered his situation with the police. In a soft voice, she said, "We heard about the police and all...the case..." She bit back the rest of her words.

Donny straightened and adjusted his cap. "Oh, that," he began. With an edge in his voice, he described the details the county police had taken regarding the stalking case against him. "But when they got their act together, they realized I was no stalker." He shrugged. "And I'm not." He rubbed the back of his neck.

"What a relief. I'm so happy for you," she said, holding her hands together under her chin as though about to pray.

"Yep, sure is," he said with a nod.

"Listen. I was hoping to find you," she began.

"Don't tell me you're having car troubles again." He shielded his eyes from the sun. "Where's your car?"

"Oh, no, not today." She chuckled. "Hey, do you have a minute, or are you on your way to pick up someone?"

"Nope, just waiting on dispatch is all."

"Good," she said, taking him by the arm. "There's something Brian and I want to ask you."

****

"This looks familiar," Brian said as they drove along the winding road through the park.

"It should. It's where the annual fair came to town

every year," Lissa said, pointing to the field where a covered bridge spanned a small stream in the distance. "They're called *kissing* bridges, those old covered bridges from back in the 19th century."

Brian slowed the car and pulled over onto the overlook as the girls pressed their noses up against the windows.

"There was a legend in town about them. Apparently, they said that in Pinewood, more people fell in love there than in any other town in Maryland after they'd driven over one."

"Sweet," Lacy said.

"And wherever Cupid's arrow fell, the kindling it stirred would simmer forever."

She caught Brian's eye.

"You wanna get married *here?*" he asked.

Lissa smiled. "I can't think of a better place."

"I like it, Mom," Lacy piped in.

"Me, too," chimed Hannah.

Chapter Forty-Nine

Melodious strains of Mendelssohn filtered in the still September air of Glen Meadows Park. Gathered in the grassy clearing at the foot of the Lora Loch Bridge sat several rows of white wooden chairs all draped in pastel shades of blue, pink, and yellow ribbons. Clusters of pale pink roses hung along the aisles and also adorned the arbor at the front of a low stone wall.

"Wow, aren't you a sight," said Uncle Charlie, who wrapped his arms around Lissa and planted a kiss lightly on her cheek. "Sorry, we're late. Your aunt had a run in her stocking. I hope you weren't too worried." The faint scent of amber drifted from his skin.

"She always worries," Lacy chimed in.

"Never mind, Lacy. Uncle Charlie, you look amazing. Not to worry. You're here, now. And I'm sure Aunt Celia's stockings look amazing, too." Lissa raised her hand to block the sun as she turned to the guests who were gathering on the hill. "Where is she?"

"She's here. Somewhere," he said, adjusting his tie.

Lissa smoothed her hands nervously down the folds of her silk dress and took a peek from where she stood beside the bridge. Her heart palpitated when, oddly, she couldn't find Brian anywhere in the crowd. She searched the rows, one-by-one, and spotted Robin, little Alex, Aunt Celia, and Miss Rucker seated together. Behind them sat Mrs. Houser, Drew, and some other neighbors and friends from church, along with Dr. Billing and his wife. Coming up in the near distance, she spotted Cousin Lenny, and her nephew, Stephen. The rest of the gathering consisted of Brian's parents and other relatives from his side of the family. *Where's Brian?*

Her heart thudded in her chest as she scanned the crowd. By the time she took another look, the sun emerged from behind a tassel of clouds and, in the distance, she finally spotted him chatting with the pastor. Her heart lightened. Next to them, stood their best man, Donny McCall, who cleaned up so well she hardly recognized him.

Lacy and Hannah, adorable in their ivory lace dresses, busied themselves comparing each other's basket of roses.

"Okay, girls, it's almost time." She clapped her hands to get their attention. "Let's get ourselves centered."

"What's centered?" Hannah asked.

"It means to calm down and focus," Lacy interjected. "Just breathe in through your nose and out through your mouth and hold your finger and thumb like this." Lacy demonstrated the exercise until Hannah caught on. "My mom does this all the time."

Lissa paused to say a quick, silent prayer. Moments later, the processional music began.

"All right, very good, girls," Lissa said, pulling her daughter's hands away from her face and quickly fixing her hair. "I think we're calm enough. Now it's time to head out. You know what you're doing, right?"

"Got it, Mom. We practiced it enough." She rolled her eyes.

I hope so.

From the hill, she watched the girls walk together and scatter the rose petals along the white runner. Uncle Charlie gave her a wink and then took her by the hand and placed it on his arm before they headed down the aisle.

With all the memories she made as a young child contributing to the blueprint of her life, there would always be a piece of her heart attached to this place. The defining moments pressed into the far reaches of her psyche, no less than a notary seal on a civil document. What better place to seal the covenant of her love with her childhood friend than right here. Her moment had come. In a few minutes she would be Mrs. Brian Pickering. Her heart felt so light, the late September breeze could have carried it away. At the altar, Uncle Charlie let go of her arm, kissed her on the cheek, and placed her hand in Brian's.

Lissa leaned into Brian, perfectly calm in his presence, much the same as she'd been even as a little girl. After their vows, Pastor DuBow closed his Bible and gave Brian a subtle grin, saying, "You may now kiss the bride." After a warm, sweet kiss, they turned around and the pastor announced to the crowd, "May I now introduce Mr. and Mrs. Brian Lawrence Pickering."

The scattered clouds parted, and the sun shone full as the smiling couple moved down the aisle hand-in-hand. In the crowd, an unexpected face in the last row drew her attention. There sat Brian's eldest daughter, Madison. Her face held a reserved smile. Even though Lissa forgave her for what happened, she never expected the girl to show up at the wedding. Another answered prayer.

The coo of mourning doves echoed from the birch trees. Lissa looked toward the sky. In that moment, two birds flew out from the trees and landed on top of the kissing bridge. A small voice spoke inside of her. She'd heard it before, and her heart ached with bittersweet joy at the memory. The words belonged to Jason and served as a reminder of something he once told her before he went off to Afghanistan for another tour of duty. He had given her permission to remarry if anything were to happen to him. She chided him at the time and didn't believe his remark all that humorous. Now, she couldn't help smiling at the memory of his words: *"Maybe, one day, you'll get to marry Brian Pickering after all."*

A word about the author...

Servant of the King of Kings, Mary adopted her natural love of language early—right after her third-grade teacher told her parents their daughter would never become a mathematician.

After earning a B.A. in English Writing and Communications, she eventually became a radio/TV broadcaster in Philadelphia. After sixteen years in the news biz, she began writing full time and hasn't stopped. *Beyond the Roses* is her third novel.

http://www.marycantell.com

57492085R00146

Made in the USA
Columbia, SC
09 May 2019